What Every Girl Should Know

What Every Girl Should Know

Margaret Sanger's Journey

a novel by
J. Albert Mann

A
atheneum

New York   London   Toronto   Sydney   New Delhi

An imprint of Simon & Schuster Children's Publishing Division
1230 Avenue of the Americas, New York, New York 10020

For information about special discounts for bulk purchases, please contact Simon & Schuster Special Sales at 1-866-506-1949 or business@simonandschuster.com.
The Simon & Schuster Speakers Bureau can bring authors to your live event. For more information or to book an event, contact the Simon & Schuster Speakers Bureau at 1-866-248-3049 or visit our website at www.simonspeakers.com.
Book design by Sonia Chaghatzbanian and Irene Metaxatos
The text for this book was set in ITC Slimbach Std.
Manufactured in the United States of America
First Edition
10 9 8 7 6 5 4 3 2 1
Library of Congress Cataloging-in-Publication Data
Names: Mann, Jennifer Ann, author.
Title: What every girl should know : Margaret Sanger's journey : a novel / by J. Albert Mann.
Description: First edition. | New York : Atheneum, [2019] | Summary: In this fictionalized biography, a teenage Maggie Higgins struggles to balance her responsibilities to her family, society's expectations for women, and her desire to pursue her education and plan for the future. | Includes bibliographical references.
Identifiers: LCCN 2018017991 (print) | LCCN 2018024927 (eBook)
ISBN 9781534419346 (eBook) | ISBN 9781534419322 (hardcover)
Subjects: LCSH: Sanger, Margaret, 1879-1966—Childhood and youth—Juvenile fiction. | CYAC: Sanger, Margaret, 1879-1966—Childhood and youth—Fiction. | Family life—New York (State)—Fiction. | Schools—Fiction. | Sex role—Fiction. | New York (State)—History—19th century—Fiction.
Classification: LCC PZ7.M31433 (eBook) | LCC PZ7.M31433 Wh 2019 (print)
DDC [Fic]—dc23
LC record available at https://lccn.loc.gov/2018017991

To my daughter,
Grace Magdalene Mann

What Every Girl Should Know

March 1, 1899

I arrive on time for the earliest train with everything I own: a valise carrying two dresses, three pairs of knickers, a nightgown, and my silk gloves—all neatly folded and packed. My coat is buttoned to my chin to keep out the raw cold of early spring. My boots are laced up tightly. My hair is braided. My face is washed. Anyone witnessing my clipped stride as I enter Trenton Station would agree that I look like someone who is prepared to board a train. And I am prepared to board a train . . . I think.

They say my mother is dying—again. I don't believe it. In truth I suspect I'm being rushed home to save my father from a sink full of dirty dishes. Although I understand his confusion: According to this world, a man confronted with the prospect of washing his own burnt saucepan is considered to be in quite dire circumstances. Either way, I have been summoned.

I admit I don't regret having to leave my teaching job in New

Jersey. It hadn't turned out as I'd expected. Or rather it turned out exactly as I'd expected, though I'd held out hope for the contrary. I wanted to believe that once inside the classroom, I'd discover the joy in educating children, as so many others had before me. But I didn't. The four walls of the classroom felt like a trap. The repetition of information, another trap. Unfortunately, what choice did I have but to teach? The same choice I now have to return home to clean the kitchen. Not only are women reduced to marry, maid, or schoolmarm, but men seem to be in control of which one we get to do at any moment.

I make my way toward the platform, dodging fellow passengers while my ears are assaulted by the echo of gate announcements. Leaving is the right thing to do. Going home is the right thing to do. And so I am bound for Corning, New York.

A whistle shrieks. My train appears as a silent flash of light, and I move to pick up my bag, dipping unsteadily since I'd never placed it down. The glint glows brighter and brighter, and is followed by a faint, far-off rumbling like a growing storm. The rumble grows into a roar, until it feels as if the massive engine barreling down on the station will drive straight through my ribs, slicing me in two. I close my eyes, welcoming the dissection . . . imagining half of me flung high up over the tracks and spinning off unfettered into the city's morning rush, while the other half, flattened and stiff, marches itself aboard the train. They truly only need half of me at home. In fact, they'd all be happier with half, as long as it is the half that cooks and cleans without complaint. But who am I fooling, there isn't the smallest piece of me able to do these things without complaint. I'm more afraid of that burnt saucepan than my father is.

The platform shakes as my train thunders into the station, and though I plant my boots firmly on the platform, I can't stop my entire body from shaking with it. Car after car after car hurtles by. At last the metal wheels squeal to a stop, sounding like a giant tea kettle going off, and the deafening hiss of steam that I'd been anticipating, nevertheless sends my heart skidding. The doors rattle and then open with a disappointing thud.

The platform erupts with sound and movement—a flurry of faces, voices, and trunks. People flow from the opened doors of the train like a colorful river, bobbing and cascading toward the staircases. Others pool around the doors waving tickets, clamoring to board.

I should get on.

Almost as suddenly as it started, the commotion slows. Trunks are hauled away. Passengers settle into their seats. The conductor, a heavyset man wearing a too-tight blue uniform, walks the length of three train cars in either direction giving everyone a last chance to disembark or board.

I *really* should get on.

My eyes fix on the open train door, a portal promising to whisk me away from my recent failure . . . only to drop me directly on the front steps of all my old ones.

I'm the only one left on the platform. The conductor glances my way. I see a spark of recognition in his eyes. He must remember me from yesterday morning. Or possibly the morning before that. But it's not his business whether or not I get on the train, and the annoyed expression on his face makes this perfectly clear as he grants me one more moment to decide.

Deep inside I hear her. My mother. *Margaret Louise,* she says. It's all she says. But it means so many things. *Stop fooling around. This is the way it is. Get on the train.*

The First Time

I rushed as fast as I could up the hill with two words on my mind. *For Mother.*

In Corning, New York, everywhere was uphill. And cold. Corning was always cold. In 1878—the winter before I was born—thermometers dipped to twelve below. Corningites liked to call the eleven winters since then "spring." It was only a good joke when you weren't freezing to death.

"Maggie!"

At the sound of my little sister Ethel's voice I stopped and turned. I was a block and a half ahead of her. Behind her paraded the boodle of my brothers and sisters. I refused to wait. Partly because standing still meant frostbite, but mostly because of those two lovely words written in my best script on the first page of my wildflower report tucked safely in between my books. Five miles was a long way to walk uphill. But it was also a long way to be alone with my own gloriously uninterrupted thoughts about my marvelous report with its neatly printed grade of A+ and its detailed description of every single wildflower in the whole of Steuben County.

I didn't care one red bean about wildflowers, or any flowers for that matter. But luckily I hadn't yet chosen a subject for my report when Miss Hayes mentioned that it should include a dedication page. And after she did, I immediately chose wildflowers to please my mother. I could have chosen taxes to please my father, but my father was so often pleased.

Being happily occupied with my dedication, I barely noticed the wind biting my ears or the endless frozen slog. I was almost home when my brother Thomas slid in beside me carrying Ethel, now sound asleep on his back, her spit drooling down his neck. I couldn't believe he was able to catch up to me hauling a load like my little sister.

"What's up, goop?" he asked.

I didn't answer his insult, but I did snatch the books from his hands, making it easier for him to carry her, and we trudged the last mile home listening to each other panting in the freezing air. My thoughts dimmed considerably as they turned from my report to my chores, and my toes felt as though they might snap off at any moment.

We picked up our pace at the sight of our chimney smoke. The dogs caught our scent and barked wildly from their pens. Thomas hollered at them to hush, waking Ethel, who pulled her head from his warm back and complained, only to drop it back against him a moment later, solidly asleep.

After another few steps, Thomas and I slowed to a stop and glanced at each other. It was quiet. Too quiet. Where were the little ones, Clio and Henry? Usually they were outside playing at this time, no matter how cold and gray it was. My mother liked her children hearty. She also liked her house clean.

Thomas and I stood in the gloom waiting for Joseph, Mary, Nan, and John to catch up to us. Joseph was the second oldest Higgins; Mary, the first. He and Mary were the living, breathing definition of fortitude and strength. Nan and John came next, born less than a year apart from each other. They were the kindest of us. We called them our heart. Then came Thomas, me, and Ethel. No one knew what to call us.

"What?" Joe asked, his cheeks red from the climb and the cold.

Thomas shrugged. Something seemed wrong. We looked around at one another and then at the house. . . . We all felt it now.

"Let's go," Mary whispered.

She took the lead. Thomas and I hung back, as if our birth order made it necessary to allow the older ones to overtake us. Ethel snored against Thomas.

The closer to the cabin we got, the more my ears seemed stuffed with worry. I could no longer hear the wind clicking through the empty elm branches or the scratchy breath fogging from my mouth. When Mary opened our front door, the sound was released, and it rolled over me in a wave: Henry wailing from his crib, Clio whimpering from the floor in a messy diaper, our wet boots hammering across the floorboards to my parent's bedroom door. And then screaming. My screaming.

"Get her outside," Mary commanded.

Joseph had already shoved past me on his way to the barn for the horse. He was going for Father at his shop in town. John grabbed hold of me, trying to calm me down, trying to pull me out of my mother's bedroom. But I wouldn't listen or stop screaming. That is until Thomas yanked me off my feet, carried me to the front door, and tossed me out into the snow like a bucket of dirty sink water. I hit face first, busting open my lip. Scrambling up out of the wet cold, I threw myself at the door just as he slammed it in my face. The bolt slid shut with a snap.

Ethel hugged me from behind, sobbing. They had put her out as well. I shoved her off me and howled at the door, attacking it with my fists, pounding so hard the boards bounced back at my hands as if they were alive.

Thomas unlatched it and swung it wide, his fury burning so much hotter than my own that it knocked the air right out of me.

"Back off, you relentless little rag!"

I stumbled backward as he slammed the door and bolted it again.

I sniffed in cold snot, and with it, the smell of blood. My school books were scattered around my feet, the pages of my report tumbling away across the snow. I hated wildflowers.

Placing both my hands on the door, I leaned my forehead against the wood, not knowing what to do. Until I remembered the window.

I snatched up the wash bucket and raced around to her window, where I flipped the bucket upside down and . . . stopped.

What did I want so badly to see?

Not what I'd already seen.

My mother. Lying in her bed silent and still, her long braid neatly plaited and resting over her shoulder, looking very much like it had been carefully placed there. The covers pulled up and over her mountain of a stomach. And Mrs. O'Donnell, on her knees next to the bed, praying. People only prayed if someone was dying, or already dead.

I hopped up on the bucket and I saw it again.

"Mother," I whispered, so lightly the word didn't fog the glass.

Why wasn't she coughing? She was always coughing. Why wasn't she coughing now? Where was the sweat and moaning of labor? The contractions? The blood? The pain?

The only movement in the room was Mrs. O'Donnell's praying lips, reciting prayers to a god my father said didn't exist. I raised my fists to shatter the glass into a thousand pieces. To stop her lips. To stop her prayers. But Ethel was standing behind me, clinging to the end of my skirt. And my mother . . . she liked the praying.

I lowered my hands and stared through the glass, willing her to see me. Willing her to live.

Mrs. O'Donnell turned toward the bedroom door. Mary and Nan entered. They were carrying a basin and rags.

No!

I leaped from the barrel, tearing myself from Ethel.

No! No! No!

Were they going to cut the baby from her? But she wasn't dead. You didn't cut babies from live mothers, because when you did, they died. I was back at the door. Pounding again. My screeches so loud I didn't hear the horse. Or their footsteps.

I was plucked from my feet and twirled in the air into his arms.

"Margaret, what a fuss you're making."

Father!

I clutched him round his neck, smothering my face in his long red hair. Joseph shouted for John to open the door. I heard the snap of the bolt and the squeak of the hinges, and I was dropped from my father's arms. He walked in and the door shut behind him.

I slipped to my knees into the snow and leaned heavily against the side of the cabin. Ethel crawled onto my lap, still crying.

"It's okay," I soothed. "He will save her."

Best Laid Plans

Consumption. A disease snacking slowly on her insides. Each tiny bite causing her to cough. And cough. Unless she didn't cough. And this was so much worse.

The doctor said rest cures consumption. But with nine children and a tenth still on the way, there was only rest if you were dead. And my mother was not dead, my father had seen to that. Though she might yet be dying.

My father sat by her side telling her jokes, reading her poetry, and sneaking sips of whiskey between her lips when she'd let him, his remedy for every ill. I pranced in with a pun now and then. *If you're going through hell, keep going.* My mother always smiled weakly before whispering for me to return to my chores. Mary stayed behind from school to do the cooking and cleaning and washing, and of course to care for Clio and Henry.

Morning after morning we left for school carrying the worry of what might happen while we were gone. And each afternoon we returned to find her alive was like that wonderful feeling of pulling off your boots after a long walk. But the happy release didn't last long because she was not getting better. She was not coughing.

Our house was suspended in a strange quiet, as quiet as a two-room cabin can be with eleven people shuffling about under its roof. Sometimes the babies cried, but Mary or Nan quickly shushed them. We were all busy listening for the sound of her returning health. Any one of us would have given a bucket of gold to hear her cough. Just one single dry, rasping cough. The winter turned colder, and the coal bin lighter.

"I'm worried about the baby," Nan whispered across the pillow during an especially long night of silence.

"I couldn't care less about that nasty little Higgins eating away at her in there," I said.

Nan gasped. And Mary whispered my name in wonder from across the dark room. Ethel was sound asleep, as usual.

But I didn't care. Even if these babies did turn into siblings I loved, first they took pieces of her, pieces we never got back. Even the ones that didn't make it. Especially the ones that didn't make it.

"Admit it," I said, "babies are ugly, bleating little goats."

Nan gasped again.

"Oh, stop gasping," I snarled. "You're always gasping."

"Maggie!" Nan gasped. But then she clapped her hand over her mouth. "I'm a gasper," she solemnly acknowledged, and she laughed—a tinkling, high-pitched, happy giggle. And as if the joy of Nan's laugh ringing out in the night cracked open the silence, my mother coughed.

Nan and I reached for each other over the top of Ethel, clasping hands.

"Did you hear it, Mary?" I asked.

Mary shushed me from her bed by the window. But she heard it. And now the three of us listened together.

She coughed again.

The opera in Paris couldn't sound more beautiful than my mother's cough.

The next morning after fetching two buckets of water to fill the dry sink for Mary, I hurried to my mother's bedroom door to see how she was feeling. I found her sitting up in bed nursing Henry, Ethel curled up alongside her.

"Ethel," I yelled, completely forgetting about my mother. "It was your turn to fill the sink."

"Don't be cross with her, Margaret Louise," my mother whispered. "She's just a baby."

"Yes, Mother," I said. But she wasn't a baby. And the one person who should know this better than anyone was my mother.

Mary hustled into the room, a cup of steaming tea in one hand and Clio in the other. She stopped and dropped the baby into my arms. "He needs a fresh diaper." And then she placed the tea down on my mother's bedside table, whisking up the old cup from yesterday in the next motion. My mother's eyes landed on my older sister, soft with approval. It was a look Mary was so used to receiving, she didn't even notice it.

"Mother," I said. "I hope you . . ."

Clio jammed his wet thumb up my nose. I yanked it out and was instantly overcome by a horrific whiff of his diaper. Holding him as far away as possible, I still couldn't stop myself from gagging.

"Margaret Louise," my mother sighed, and she turned her

back to me as she moved Henry to her other breast. That was it. Just my name. But I understood her full meaning. *It's a dirty diaper. A simple task. What is wrong with you?*

I watched Ethel wiggle in closer to her, and though I was only five feet away, I could hardly imagine crossing the distance to the bed.

Clio shrieked. I hitched him higher on my hip and trudged off to the wash bucket.

I have never understood why we called them dirty diapers. Dirt smelled rich and clean, like it had captured both the sun and the rain and shaken them up into the most beautiful potion out of which grew everything from sweet alyssum to yellow violets and painted trillium. All three of which I'd featured in my wildflower report. Clio's diaper was not filled with dirt.

I breathed through my mouth as I wiped him clean with cold water from the bucket. He screamed and twisted away from me. Trying not to be cross with him, I begged him through clenched teeth to stay still. If only Mary had handed me Henry. Henry was so much more cooperative.

"Cold, cold, c-cold," Clio stuttered.

Nan saved me, stepping in to finish the job, and I rushed over to the bucket next to the sink filled with breakfast dishes to wash my hands. The water there was also cold. Everything was cold. Everywhere was cold.

From the bedroom came the sound of coughing. And then more coughing. It was amazing how quickly her cough had fallen from the coveted melody it was last night to its usual rank of plain old sickness. As I scrubbed my hands, I made a silent vow to be the very first to her bedside after school . . . before Ethel could wiggle in her skinny little caboose.

Spotting me near the sink, Mary smiled. "Wonderful, Maggie," she said. "Thank you. Once you're finished with the dishes, you should hurry or you'll be late to school."

"But it's not my turn . . . ," I started to argue, but she was clearly gone, and so I began the darned dishes.

Thomas dropped his oatmeal bowl in the sink with a smirk.

"I hate you," I whispered.

He popped me one on the top of my head.

I went after him, soapy hands and all, but my father came between us. "Enough playtime. There is work to be done," he bellowed in his jolly way as he dropped his dirty bowl into what had sadly become my sink full of dirty dishes. "Now let me feel that head." His big hands massaged where Thomas had bruised me through my thick auburn hair.

"This," he said, "is the head of a fine surgeon."

He always said this.

My father was a practiced phrenologist: someone who believed the shape and size of our skulls revealed our character, our skills, and our abilities. By trade, he was a sculptor, chipping away at blocks of marble until a beautiful angel emerged, destined to decorate the headstone of a rich Roman Catholic or Protestant of Corning. But to chisel each individual cherub's likeness, he studied the skull, or phrenology.

Father believed the head was the sculptured expression of the soul. How wide-set the eyes, the shape of the ridge between them, a turned-up nose, how full or thin the lips, bulges in front of or behind the ears—all had meaning. A researcher had to be inquisitive, with curiosity bumps along the back of his cranium; a musician needed to have order and time over his eyebrows; and a brilliant doctor must possess the proper protuberances around the ears, which I had, as Father always said proudly. So, I would be a doctor. Because of my large protuberances. And the first thing I'd do was cure my mother.

Mary was right, I was late heading out for school. Not that Miss Hayes would mind. Girls were often late, and it seemed the older we got the later we became. Although this might make leaving school early to keep my vow a bit trickier this afternoon. I would have to catch up, and stay caught up, which I could surely do. I was good at school. I worked hard. Working hard at school was a requirement of a future doctor. Dr. McMichael had told me this much the day I splinted John McGill's arm using the branch that cracked off the tree when he fell from it. When I'd asked about other requirements, the doctor had laughed and said I'd get over my desire to be a doctor by that time. Out of respect, I didn't point out what a ratbag he was.

I hurried down the hill, not because I was late, but because, as usual, I was cold. The town of Corning hugged a steep hill rising up from the Chemung River. Along the river flats lived the factory workers who blew and cut the glass at Corning Glass Works. Their slouching houses were held together by laundry lines flapping with wash under which children scampered about like squirrels. The flats sat inside the black smoke belching from the furnace stacks of the factories. The hill sat above the smoke. On the hill lived the people who owned and managed the factory. Their giant houses loomed over two or three children so bundled against the cold they could barely waddle from their grand front entryways to their waiting carriage doors.

My family lived beyond the hill—in the woods alongside the Erie Railroad tracks. We weren't a part of the flats. But we also weren't a part of the hill. We were just ourselves, and a few scattered neighbors who called the woods their home.

I passed over West Fourth, my best friend Emma's street. I'm sure she was already bent over her mathematics. Protestants were never late to school. And Emma was a Protestant, her father a manager of finance at the factory. Her house on the hill was a marvel of rooms, each larger even than our attic, with ceilings twice as high and store-bought furniture everywhere. So many chairs. There was only Emma and her older brother, James, and her mother and father. Four people and a glut of places to sit. In our house, my father had made every stick of furniture, and there were considerably fewer chairs than there were Higginses. To win one, a Higgins had to arrive early and be ready to defend it, as any Higgins with a heartier punch could swiftly remove you. Thomas always sat comfortably.

I slid into school and took my seat next to Nan. The coal stove was chugging, and I felt as though my frozen body was melting as Nan explained where we were in the mathematics lesson.

I finished my figures in a dreamy state, but still long before Nan finished hers. Nan was a writer, not a mathematician. She even won a prize for a story she wrote for a children's magazine, *The Youth's Companion*, this past Christmas. Mother kept a copy of it in the drawer with her Bible, a place where I had so wanted my wildflower report to find its way. There it would have nestled next to the single pressed chicory bloom she and I had collected on a long-ago sunny spring morning. I can't remember why it had just been the two of us. I only remember that it had . . . along with the memory of the moment we came upon them. A field of bright blue, as if pieces of the sky had sprinkled down upon the greening earth. She turned to me with such joy that I instantly felt every last blossom had sprung straight from my heart.

"Let's pick them all," I'd suggested.

She had laughed, the sound of it swirling through the flowers. "No, Margaret Louise. You can't pick chicory. It won't keep. The blooms will fade to white by this afternoon," she explained. "We need to enjoy them right now."

She looked off over the field and breathed in deeply, and then she reached out and plucked a single stem. For me.

When we arrived home, she placed it gently between the pages of the Bible where it quickly turned white, just as she said it would. But I didn't listen to her advice. The sun, the flowers, her smile—I'd enjoyed them every day since.

Glancing over at Nan's work, I noticed she had passed by some of her problems. I leaned across the desk and began to help. Later, she'd do the same for my composition, correcting my grammar. Mary usually sat with us, but she didn't need any help in her subjects. She was a master of them all. If my father ever played around with Mary's head, he'd find plenty of meaningful bumps.

Over lunch I plotted my early exit from school, daydreaming about the warm position Ethel had occupied this morning. Emma was munching on hazelnuts and chatting about a new porcelain doll her mother had brought over for her from Germany. Thank goodness Nan was listening because I wasn't. Emma never grew tired of those glass-eyed demons. I found them all a bit terrifying. I blinked at her as she expounded in detail on the doll's corset, but my thoughts sailed off to my newly forming plan.

The class would end with a reading. We always did. It would be Milton's *Paradise Lost*. It always was. I despised this poem. *One woman destroys the world and sticks the rest of us with a lifetime of the bloody and painful birthing of babies? Really, that first man on Earth could have just not eaten the darned apple.* However much I hated this poem, I planned to be the first volunteer to declaim it. And when Miss Hayes called up the next reader, I would return to my seat, swipe up my books, and act as though I was heading for the necessary. Miss Hayes wouldn't stop the reading to ask questions, and I'd be out the door before Ethel could squeeze out her first whine. It was Friday. A long way from Monday and consequences. If Miss Hayes even remembered by then. My only regret was leaving the heat of the schoolhouse early because it was also a long way from Monday and a coal stove full of coal.

Every subject brought us closer to my plan. History came and went. French . . . *le même.* And just as I suspected, Milton was called forth from the shelf and I raised my hand high. Miss Hayes smiled at my enthusiasm, causing me a bit of momentary shame at my scheming. But it passed as soon as she called on me, and my plan was kicked into action.

I positioned my books, ignoring Nan's questioning glance, and trotted to the front of the class. But then Miss Hayes placed Milton back on the shelf.

"I know how much you love plays, Margaret," she said. "How about we begin *The Lady of Lyons*?"

I was thrilled to have Milton's truly blank verse replaced with such a drama! I had to admit, I was quite the orator. Even Mary agreed. She said I was versatile. And Mary should know, she adored plays, and understood more about the theater than Mr. William Shakespeare. Which was by no means an exaggeration.

I threw myself into the reading.

"This is thy palace, where the perfumed light
steals through the mist of alabaster lamps,
and every air is heavy with the sighs
of orange groves, and music from sweet lutes
and murmurs of low fountains, that gush forth
I' the midst of roses!"

When I took a breath, I heard a few snorts from the McGill brothers sitting closest to me. Thomas heard them too. My heart curled into a smile as I thought of how they would pay for those piggy noises. Thomas and I might be at each other's throats every day of our lives, but my throat was a Higgins throat. And Thomas Higgins didn't like pig noises.

I read on, lost in the love story of Princess Pauline and Claude Melnotte, the handsome son of the gardener, forgetting all about my plan until Miss Hayes stood and applauded. It was then that I realized I'd read straight through the entire first act and she was dismissing us.

First, I gave a quick bow—because it's customary to do so when receiving such thunderous applause—then I tossed the play onto her desk and dove for my books.

Everyone was scrambling into the aisles between the desks, forcing me to elbow my way through to the door, with a special jab for the closest McGill. I was almost free when there in my path stood Ethel Higgins.

"Maggie," she moaned. "Will you carry . . ."

I shoved past her, determined to let nothing get in the way of my plan. Grabbing my overcoat, I leaped down the steps, and . . . bumped right into Mary standing in Father's old kip boots, and bundled against the cold by a large scarf made of thrown-off trousers. Mary wasn't Ethel. She couldn't be shoved past.

Croup

"There's croup at the O'Donnell's," Mary reported.

"But, Mother," I said.

Mary sighed. "It's bad, Maggie."

As we headed toward our closest neighbors I formed a new plan. Because I was versatile. Once we hit the split in the road between our house and the O'Donnell's, I'd ask Mary's permission to turn for home to start the potatoes for dinner. Mary would grant it, given that I wasn't often excited about cooking. All was not lost.

But then it was.

Right before we hit the fork in the road, Mary asked Nan to head home and begin the potatoes. I wanted to argue but didn't. I was the future doctor, so I should be tending the sick. Not Nan. Nan was the writer. And she always said she did her best writing while she mended and peeled. I watched my sister head for home, my heart warm with self-sacrifice for allowing her to go without argument. Although within ten paces, I was freezing again and my heart was as cold as the rest of me.

When we turned onto the rutted track that led to the O'Donnell's, Mary made another awful announcement. "Father said to bring any healthy children home with us."

"But there are a hundred of them," I blurted.

"There are eleven, Maggie," Mary said.

I knew very well how many O'Donnells there were. This wasn't the point. But the point didn't matter. Now all my cold heart could muster was not wishing illness on a herd of O'Donnell children while trying even harder not to envision my dinner plate with a solitary spoonful of Nan's boiled cabbage and potatoes.

My stomach rumbled.

Our dinners were spread pretty thin across Father's marble-topped table, even if you weren't rounding up a dozen O'Donnells to squeeze around it, and tomorrow's breakfast was a long way off.

"Are they staying the night?" I asked, not hiding my gloom.

"Children need to be looked after and fed, and we can't expect Mrs. O'Donnell to do it when she's tending to her sick ones, can we, Margaret Louise?"

It's what my mother called me. Mary used it to remind me of my duty, but all it did was vex me. If it were Ethel, I'd tell her to shut her saucebox, but you didn't say that kind of thing to Mary. Instead I asked as sweetly as I could, "What about expecting ugly Mr. O'Donnell to do it?"

Mary didn't answer. Instead, she walked faster, leaving me to think about my words. I sped up and kept pace, leaving my words to think about themselves.

* * *

The O'Donnell's yard was littered with wash buckets, laundry baskets, garbage, pigs, and little O'Donnells, who dashed about between the pigs while the laundry laid wrinkled and wet in its baskets.

"Laundry's not hung," I said before I could stop myself, and then cringed in the moment of silence that followed, hoping upon hope Mary didn't suggest I hang it.

"I'll hang it," Ethel said, turning toward the laundry without even throwing me a sour look for not offering to help, which really peeved me. What a lickfinger. Mother wasn't even here to see her doing the right thing. And Mary seeing it didn't count. Although Mary *did* throw me a puckered look, which I pretended I didn't see. It was bad enough I was forced to pin Thomas's underwear to the line every day of my life; not even the croup would get me pinning up O'Donnell underwear. And when Mary headed for the house, I was right on her boots.

It was dark inside, as the late afternoon sun seemed unable to cram itself through the only window next to the cookstove. Mr. O'Donnell rocked a toddler in his lap inside the door. His red-rimmed, glassy eyes landed on us like a nervous fly. At first it looked like he might be corned, but I realized he was sick. Real sick. His neck was thick and his breath a rasp. Now my words caught up to me, and though it was truthful he was ugly, I felt terrible about him being so ill.

Mary reached out and eased the sleeping heap of rags from his lap. He allowed her to take the little one, dropping his empty arms with a sigh.

Like our own house, there was only one other room besides the kitchen. This door was open, and Mrs. O'Donnell shuffled out. Although I could tell right away she didn't have the croup, she looked worse than Mr. O'Donnell. Exhausted and pregnant.

"I won't hug you, Mary," she said, her arms hanging limply at her side. "But know I'd like to."

"No need, Mrs. O'Donnell," my sister responded. "Go lie down and rest. We'll get things in order here before we take the little ones." This was a hint for me to get to work.

I knew exactly where to begin, as croup was as common as fleas in fall. I searched out a water bucket and headed out to the well. The hoarse barking of croup dried out the throat. Cool water soothed it. This, and a wet cloth to the forehead, would bring down the fever. I'd let Mary comfort. She was an expert at it. Like my father, I was better at treatment. Although my curative measures left out whiskey, but only because I wasn't allowed to carry a flask around with me as he did.

Once I'd watered the sick and helped Mary set up and light the croup kettles, the only things left were the dirty dishes and the diaper bucket brimming with a dark mess of diapers. I chose the dishes, even though I knew I'd eventually have to plunge my hands into that diaper bucket. I picked my way back to the sink with fresh water, stepping over rags, boots, coats, shoes, and whatnot. Peering down into the pile of dishes, I didn't bother to wait for my eyes to adjust to the dark. Best to just start scrubbing. Which I did, for a very long time, while I listened to Mary continue to stem the misery that was croup. Lastly, I tackled the diapers. But even if my heart had finally found its way to the right place, nothing could stop the smell of those diapers from tossing my stomach around.

I was out pinning the clean diapers to the line when Mary and Ethel stumbled onto the front porch. Mary began the collection of healthy O'Donnells. She and Ethel would then start for home.

Not only was I being left to finish hanging laundry, but I'd also be the very last to enter our house tonight, breaking my vow to be the first to my mother's bedside. Served me and my slow-moving cold heart right.

"Edwin," I heard Mary say to the O'Donnell's oldest. "Why don't you stay back to help your mother."

Edwin was almost fourteen, and he gave Mary a sour frown for instructing him. If it had been Thomas, I'd have knocked him one for that look. Mary didn't seem to notice.

My sisters headed down the dusky road with their charges. I tried not to stare too longingly after them. Although a few steps later, Mary called back over her shoulder. "Maggie, come along. Edwin can finish the hanging."

I quickly caught up to the crowd in the growing dark. Happy. Even if my heart was mostly cold as ice and the only thing waiting at home was a herd of dirty little O'Donnell feet to wash before bed.

March 1, 1899

The wagon hits a rut and I accidentally whack my brother in the head with the umbrella. Thomas throws me a black look.

"Whoops." I shrug.

I swear he's purposely steering our old horse into every rut in the street.

"You know I was here yesterday," he grumps.

"I know."

"And the day before."

"I know," I say more forcefully.

I expected my brother to be angry. And I probably deserve more grief than he's giving me, but I'm annoyed anyway, and I can't keep it out of my tone.

"You're not right in the head, Maggie Higgins. Do you know that?"

I tighten my grip on the umbrella. I'm not right in the head, and I do know it. But it's not from lack of trying. Why doesn't life ever give you anything for trying?

I can't help envisioning my mother lying in her sick bed. What has life given *her*? And she's done a heap more than try.

I sigh. "I'm here, aren't I?"

"Where else would you be?" he scoffs.

Thomas Higgins. My personal undertaker . . . his words dragging me deep into the dirt. *Where else, indeed.* But though my body may be bumping around in this broken-down wagon, my head can't seem to accept it. Do I tell him I've imagined a hundred other places to be? Do I tell him I always believed I was on my way to one of these places?

No.

Because then I'd have to admit I don't even know where these places are, or why I want to head to them.

Becoming a doctor had always been the dream. And even if it had been more my father's dream than my own, I'd been fine with his choice. Because *doctor* had really just been a word to stand in for the feeling of being or doing something important, which has sat in my stomach all my life. Which still sits in my stomach, even as Thomas makes the turn off Market Street.

But if I told my brother this . . . that I ache to *be* and *do*, I think Thomas Higgins's head might explode all over the wet street.

He glances at me and then back at the road. "Pull yourself together, Maggie."

Yes, my irritable undertaker, it is my head that's exploding. It is my insides that won't stop jangling around like a loose harness. It is my legs that are itching to leap from this wagon and run.

But like Thomas said . . . where would I go?

Escape Is Impossible

A month of O'Donnells.

Thirty-one straight days of forty arms and forty legs swinging about the house. More than two hundred fingers reaching for bread at dinner and two hundred toes to be covered by blankets at night. More than twenty mouths flapping out noise and huffing in all the air. And when I opened my eyes on Saturday morning, I was completely unable to stomach day thirty-two.

It was easy to get lost in a crowd. This I knew all too well. I dressed quickly, threw on my coat and boots, and made my escape.

A stiff breeze had my eyes watering as I passed by the necessary. Even this early in the morning a line had already formed. There wasn't enough coal ash in the world to tamp down the awful smell in that outhouse. My mother would choke if she knew I'd been peeing in the woods like an animal. But the active bowels of twenty Higginses and O'Donnells had made it necessary.

I was scrambling past the barn when my father caught sight of me. I froze. Would he stop me? Call me back? Send me inside to my chores? But he did none of these things. Instead, he gave me a knowing wink, and with permission given, I took off like a jackrabbit for Emma's, where it would be quiet. And warm.

I knocked on Emma's large front door, using the iron knuckles hanging there for just this purpose. I loved these knuckles. At home we had to use our very own skin-and-bone knuckles to get our door to open, and when it did open, it wasn't opened by Bernadette O'Boyle in a white skirt and blue apron.

"Hello, Bernie," I said, whipping past her to get to the warmth.

"Margaret Higgins, you wait," Bernie growled. "I haven't announced you."

"Emma!" I shouted.

"Bedroom!" Emma called back.

Bernie rolled her eyes as I hopped up the wide spiral staircase, down a long red carpeted hallway past a table set with white orchids, and into Emma's bedroom.

"Shut the door."

I shut it. And then there were two heads, four arms, and four legs in a large room with one feather bed and one roaring fire . . . if you didn't count all of Emma's ridiculous dolls strewn over the floor.

"Hurry, pick her up, she's crying."

Emma used her chin to point at a half-dressed doll at her feet. She had another in her arms that she was feeding with a glass bottle.

"It's not crying," I told her.

Emma rolled her eyes. "Maggie. It's pretend. Use your imagination."

"To make a baby cry? I'd rather imagine stubbing my toe."

"Oh, Maggie," she huffed, picking up the doll and rocking it herself.

We were well past the age for dolls. But I didn't say this to Emma. Instead, I pulled her copy of *Gulliver's Travels* from the shelf and turned to our favorite chapter: the one with the pirates.

Emma didn't like to read. She liked me to read. Like Mary, Emma said I had a real talent for the dramatic. Hearing I had a talent for anything made me yearn to hear it even more.

Less than a page into my reading, Emma forgot all about her fake babies, letting them roll from her lap. One laid face down on the carpet and the other on its side with one of its arms bent back; both were as quiet as turtles sunning on a log, unlike real babies.

When the story heated up, Emma reached out for the twisted-back arm of the doll, picking it up by its tiny hand. She twisted off its arm as she listened to me read, her eyes staring far off . . . imagining marauding pirates. Miss Hayes called this "dramatic tension." By the end of the chapter, Emma had twisted all the arms and legs off her dolls and was peering inside them.

I closed the book.

"What are you doing?"

"I'm seeing how they're put together," she said. "Look here, how this one twists on like a screw but this one pops into place through this notch."

"And the head?"

"The same as the arms and legs. Let's see how their eyes work."

She popped one out and it cracked. We looked at each other

and laughed. "Let me try the other one." But before she could figure out how to remove it without breaking it, her mother knocked and entered.

Six eyes met. Six eyes took in the scene. Two of them narrowed.

"Emma!" Her mother cried. "Why are you breaking your dolls?"

Emma jumped up from the floor. I jumped with her, not wanting to be left sitting among the strewn body parts.

"I'm seeing how they're made. What they look like on the inside."

Her mother's face didn't soften. This wasn't a good enough answer. "You're supposed to care for them. Not destroy them."

"But I haven't destroyed them. Well, the one eye, yes, but look, Mother," Emma explained. "See how they pop back in using the notch. Good as new."

Her mother was not convinced. "And when you have real children? Will you pop *them* back together?"

"Perhaps she won't have real children," I theorized, stepping in to help. "Perhaps Emma will teach, like Miss Hayes. Emma is the best at mathematics in the whole school."

Emma was not really the best at mathematics, more like third or fourth best, which was still pretty good. But Nan wouldn't have minded me telling a thumper, especially at a time like this, when it seemed very needed.

Emma's mother shocked me with a deepening frown. "It's time for your guest to be leaving. Please see her out."

Was there not a mother in the world I could please? All I had suggested was that Emma might teach—a teacher being a perfectly acceptable alternative to being a mother, as far as I could tell. And one of the only ways possible to keep oneself from being surrounded by crying babies. At least school-aged children wiped their own noses. Well, maybe not the McGills, but most of the rest of us did.

Emma walked me to her front door.

"I'm sorry," I told her.

She looked behind her and then whispered, "It's not your fault. I took them apart."

"But I read an exciting tale, and got you into breaking things."

"It was exciting," she admitted. "You're so dramatic."

I couldn't help smiling. I was dramatic.

Everything felt better.

But then Emma sighed. "Last month, we came home from visiting my aunt in Utica, and James had taken apart the cookstove. The whole cookstove! The legs, the ash pan, the baffles . . . all of it laid about the kitchen floor and across the dining table. Knobs and screws as far as the eye could see. And do you know what my mother said? She said, 'Oh, James, how clever of you.'"

"Was he able to put it back together?" I asked.

"Of course not! Father had to call Mr. Murdoch."

We burst out laughing.

I gave my friend a hug. "I thought your discoveries of the doll body were amazing."

"I knew you would, Maggie Higgins. But I think you might be the only one."

"But you thought so too," I reminded her.

She nodded as she closed the door, but somehow it felt as if she wasn't so sure her discoveries were amazing after all. And strangely, her words became true . . . I was the only one. Turning away from those iron knuckles on the door, I wondered what I'd find if I could pop off one of my limbs and peek inside. Would I look like all the other dolls?

There was nowhere to go but home, and so I turned toward it. Five paces in I felt the cold. Six paces in I remembered the O'Donnells. No notched and screwed arms and legs waiting there. They were all real. Every last eyeball. Along with my mother's eyeballs, which had surely noticed me missing.

Five long miles later, I slinked past the barn and necessary, and then slipped through the front door. Not seeing my mother among the crowd, I breathed a little easier as I skittered over to the dry sink and began to wash the dishes. There were always dishes.

Comfortably settled into a chore and feeling a natural part of the din of the house, I was now prepared for her to appear. But she didn't.

And after another few moments, I became a little alarmed that I might end up washing all the dishes without her even seeing me do it. Although there really were quite a lot of dishes for some reason. Which now had me wondering what Mary or Nan had been doing all day. And where were Mary and Nan? Or my father? Or Ethel?

That's when I heard the faint wail of a baby. A newborn baby. And my heart sank.

The door to my parents' bedroom opened. Nan and Ethel emerged carrying a bucket of water sloshing with bloody rags.

"Another boy," Nan announced.

"Where were you, Maggie?" Ethel asked.

Not here. And even though the addition of another pair of arms, legs, and eyes was nothing I cared the least bit about, I couldn't believe how left out I felt. It was as if a second door had closed on me today and had left me standing all alone on the other side.

The Choice

I made a decision to never leave home again, ever . . . except for school, of course. And I'd set up camp next to the mending basket of ripped and rumpled clothes, determined to let mushrooms grow out of my ears before I moved.

Sprawled out on the floor next to my father, space being available now that the O'Donnells had finally gone, I'd been at this basket of mending every afternoon for a week. And even worse than never reaching the bottom of it, I was pretty sure my mother hadn't noticed my efforts.

"Listen to this, Margaret," my father said. He was reading *Progress and Poverty*. He was always reading *Progress and Poverty*. I'd already read Mr. George's book, as had every Higgins who could read—on a direct order from Father. Happy was the day we finished it and handed it off to the next Higgins, it being the dullest book ever written.

He cleared his voice and began. "'On the horizon the clouds

begin to lower. Liberty calls to us again. We must follow her further. We must trust her fully.'"

I rummaged through the basket while he read, looking for seams and hems, anything I could use an easy running stitch to mend. I needed a few successes to keep my spirits up.

His voice got louder, pausing at the points he wanted me to really appreciate.

"'Either we must wholly accept her or she will not stay. It is not enough that men should vote. It is not enough that they should be theoretically equal before the law. They must have liberty to avail themselves of the opportunities and means of life. . . . Either this, or Liberty withdraws her light!'"

I found a cleanly torn seam in one of my brother's trousers. I licked my fingers to wet the thread, and then slid the thread, stiff with spit, through the eye of the needle, missing it. God rot it, I hated mending!

"'Either this, or Liberty withdraws her light.'" My father slapped his knee. "What do you think of that, Margaret? Mr. George is saying that if we do not treat her right, liberty will abandon this country."

His excitement infected me. It always did. Plus, thinking about liberty was far better than thinking about trousers.

"Why is liberty always a woman, Father?" I asked. "But women don't get to vote?" I knew my question would heat him up.

"Yes, Margaret. Women should have the vote. All women. Just as black men now have the vote. How can we call ourselves free in this country when half of our good citizens are kept out of the polls? It's wrong. This is exactly what George is saying—"

"Michael." My mother interrupted.

"And here is Lady Justice, before us." My father smiled. "She will send me on an errand, I am sure."

Mother nodded wearily. She *was* sending him on an errand. When Father started in on sipping whiskey and sorting out the world's problems this early in the afternoon, he needed an errand so that the rest of us could get our work done.

"The coal money," she said. "We're nearly out and still have plenty of cold weather to get through."

My father slowly put down his book and rose from his chair. "I bid you, *adieu*, my fair Margaret," he said, bowing down at me miserably holding my needle next to the mending basket, which I swore now looked even more full than it did a moment ago. But then he glanced over at my mother's back as she consulted with Mary about what to do with the potatoes for dinner, a daily puzzle always needing solving, and we both saw the same thing. Opportunity.

I pinned my needle into the trousers and crept over Clio and Henry on my way to the door, faster than a flash of summer lightning. He scooted me out ahead of him, and then called back into the house, "Stealing Margaret for company. We'll be back before dinner," and then slammed the door shut.

Smiling, he gave my long braid a tug. "There be nothing sweeter than liberty."

I agreed. And all the way into town, he magically transformed Mr. George's dry words and endless sentences into exciting ideas that bloomed one after another. Free libraries. Free education. And his very, very favorite, freedom of the mind.

"I think I know why liberty is always a woman," I told him as we wandered down Market Street.

"Why is that, Margaret?" he asked in his Irish brogue, his

red hair blowing in the chilly breeze, and his blue eyes looking so closely into mine. He was listening. It was amazing to be listened to.

"Men are allowed to be both good and bad. But women are only allowed to be good *or* bad. And so if a woman is good, she is only good. And worthy of being something as good as freedom."

He grinned.

"But . . . ," I said, not wanting his grin to fade, not wanting to feel like I had that day I stood alone on Emma's doorstep.

"Yes?"

"I have bad in me," I admitted, dropping my eyes so I wouldn't see his disappointment. Instead, he laughed so loud it raised every hair on my bumpy head.

"Always think like this, Margaret," he bellowed. "For yourself. Always."

I quickly promised I *always* would—not caring that I wasn't sure how else I'd think. His reaction had made me feel as if I'd swallowed the moon whole, my insides glowing mysteriously.

We were passing a large display of bananas outside of Iszard's Groceries. Mr. Iszard was busy carrying them inside because it was getting late. My father plucked one up and handed it to me.

"For my Lady Liberty."

"They're two for a penny today," Mr. Iszard informed us. "They were late coming to me, and don't have much left in 'em."

"Well, well," my father said. "Now that is an honest deal, sir."

He turned to me, looking into my eyes, and then glanced up and down the busy street.

The shift was changing at the factory. Market Street was crowded with men and women trudging home, as well as young boys making their way to the evening shift. A shuffling and shouting of dark woolens against the backdrop of a muddy spring sleet, each huffing a cloud of white into the fading day.

My father stuck his hand in his pocket and pulled out the coal money, staring down at it in his open palm. The banana felt heavy in my hand.

Again, he grinned.

"My dear Lady Liberty, care to free these bananas? The choice," he said with great fanfare, "is yours."

My lips quivered. Coal or bananas. The choice was mine. But I knew the choice he was hoping I'd make. It was shining straight out from under his massive red brow. Freedom was everything. There was only one choice.

"Free them," I mumbled.

"What is that?" he laughed.

"Free the bananas!" I yelled.

And we bought them all.

The way home was a fantastic journey. We had three boxes full of overly ripe bananas. Father stacked them on top of one another and carried them on his shoulder. My job was to pick a bunch and pluck off one for the postmaster, and three for Mrs. Alterisi and her twins, and an especially large banana for Officer Cowley.

A banana for every person we passed.

People laughed at us. People laughed with us. They smiled, shook my hand . . . even hugged me. I chased the citizens of Corning up and down Market Street handing out fruit. Only old Mr. Keeler wouldn't take one.

"Foolish man," he grumbled at my father. "You're as poor as Job's turkey."

"'It is not from top to bottom that societies die,'" my father quoted Mr. George. "'It is from bottom to top.'"

Mr. Keeler waved my father away with one hand, walking off. "Can't see a hole in a ladder," he growled over his shoulder. But my father wasn't listening because we were now surrounded by a mighty swarm of children, and as he handed a banana to each child, he looked them directly in the eye and told them, "Leave the world better, because you, my child, have dwelt in it."

Every pair of eyes listened to him carefully until the banana was in their possession, and then they were off.

By the time we hit Hamilton Street, I'd eaten three bananas. My father had eaten six! We pretended our bananas were the torch of the huge statue they just finished building of Lady Liberty. She now towered over New York's harbor, a gift from the French people.

"They say the torch alone is almost thirty feet high," my father said.

I stretched out my arm and held my banana even closer to the darkening sky, and smiled so big it hurt my frozen cheeks.

When a wagon passed us on the road, we tossed three bunches of bananas to the children in the back and belly laughed at their happy screams. My father hugged me with one arm as the wagon rolled away, a brawl developing over the bananas.

"Share, citizens!" my father howled at the tail of the wagon. "Share!"

One little boy stood and saluted us. We saluted him back.

"'Let no man imagine that he has no influence,'" I sighed, quoting Mr. George.

Father tugged me closer. "Or no young woman."

Who knew fruit could change the world? Even if it was just our little corner of Corning. But the best part of bestowing bananas was not how happy it made everyone, and not how happy it made me, but how happy it made us together.

A few miles of uphill trudging and we were finally home. We entered the yard with only half a box of bananas left. It was dark. My ears and fingers burned with cold. The fruit sat in an unsettled lump at the bottom of my stomach. Lady Liberty had vanished—it was Margaret Louise Higgins who would face my mother without coal money. Or coal.

"We will be cold," she snapped. Not at him, but at me. Because I should have known better. Just as Eve should have known better in Mr. Milton's poem.

I looked to my father for help, but he had returned to his chair . . . to his book, where he would stay until he was called for dinner. Was my father the serpent or Adam? Did it matter? Men were never wrong. Only women.

I turned back toward my mother, reaching for her, because I was so sorry. So, so very sorry, and I needed her to know it, really know it. And there were no words for being so sorry you couldn't breathe.

But she hurried away to finish setting the table, leaving me trapped alone with my useless apology.

A Day of Rest

It had been raining for a week. Mud was everywhere—tracked through houses and shops, lining hems and trouser cuffs; it had even found its way into little Henry's ears.

"How'd it wind up in here?" I asked, scrubbing black mud out of his plumb red ears.

"Clio did it." He smiled.

"Oh, Henry."

Henry was my favorite, and I didn't mind saying it. He was a tiny copy of John and Nan, loving and kind. Clio was a terror. And the baby, Richard, just six months old now, was still too much tears and snot to love yet.

Since it was Sunday, Mother had the idea that all the babies should be washed, and since she was pregnant again and it was hard for her to lean over the basin, I quickly volunteered for the job. I'd been doing a lot of volunteering. It had been months since my banana mistake, and I was still working hard to correct it.

I chose to bathe Richard first because he was cleanest to start with. And Clio next, because I wanted him done. I saved Henry for last.

"Henry, who is the smartest boy in all the world?" He was playing with a rag, swishing it round him in the basin.

"I am," he said. He knew the answer without thought.

"Stand up now, silly."

I wrapped him in a towel and carried him to the cookstove where Mary was skinning rabbits, our old English setter, Toss, lying warm near her feet. She pulled a chair up close to the stove, and I sat down with Henry on my lap, his wet, sweet-smelling hair tickling my nose.

Mary broke both of a rabbit's hind legs and yanked them out of their fur, then she gathered a great handful of hide around its anus and ripped the fur straight off its body in one long, wet tug. I turned my chair so as not to see her skin the others. I loved rabbit. Especially when Mary cooked it. But I didn't love watching her tear their skins off like she was tearing up old bedsheets for rags.

Henry's warm body leaning against mine and the warmth of the cookstove had me sleepy. I closed my eyes and listened to the sounds of my mother, brothers, and sisters. Father was at his shop for the day. He always worked Sundays. Since he was an atheist, none of us attended church, including my mother. He liked to work on Sunday to prove it didn't have to be a day of rest. He took Monday for this.

My mother was a silent believer. Though she didn't take any day for rest.

"Marget," Henry said. "Tell about the house."

"Hmm," I whispered into his clean little ear. "One day," I began. "You will buy a big house."

"I will," I said.

"With plumping," he added, as usual.

"With plumbing," I corrected, as usual.

"And a special room."

"A very special room. A room that is only Henry's."

His giggles tickled my chest.

"With a featherbed."

"A big bed," he said.

"A big featherbed just for Henry and no one else."

"Specially not Clio."

I laughed. "We'll lock him right out."

"Even if he knocks and acts really nice?" Henry asked.

There was a hardy knock on the door making Henry and me jump. John answered before my mother could. It was Father Coghlan.

I immediately picked up naked little Henry and started upstairs to dress him as my mother greeted the priest, Mary put the kettle on for tea, and Nan cleared a place at the table for our guest to sit. But before he did, the priest greeted each of us by name. I said hello from up-top the stairs.

Father Coghlan spent many nights at our house chatting with Father about unions, fair wages, and better working conditions at the glass factory. Like my father, he enjoyed a bit of whiskey and a good argument. Two of my father's favorites. But my father wasn't here, and Father Coghlan knew this. He was here to speak with my mother.

My mother suggested we all join Joseph and Thomas in the barn to see if we could help with their chores.

"The barn!" I blurted. "But . . . not the babies. I just finished washing them!"

My mother never stopped smiling at the priest, but I saw the tight pull at the edges of her mouth. Disapproval. Of me. Erasing all of today's volunteering in a tiny stretch of her lips.

Nan grabbed my arm and tugged me toward the door. John swept up Ethel before she could also complain. And Mary herded out three sweet-smelling little boys who would very soon . . . not be.

The late September sun was still shining but had lost most its heat. Knowing full well Joseph and Thomas did not need our help, we headed to the barn past a long row of diapers flapping in the evening breeze.

It was dark in the barn, and smelled dusty from this past spring's brome. Mary lit a lamp and we closed the barn doors to keep the boys from going outside in the mud. Instead, they disappeared into the dirty stalls of the barn. I decided I no longer cared. Let them roll in the mud with the pigs. This was exactly why I despised housework—and babies were housework—it always came to nothing.

We could hear Thomas shouting something at Clio—everyone was always shouting at Clio. A moment later, he emerged from the interior of the barn and stared at Mary, Nan, Ethel, and me sitting on the old bales.

"How delightful to see you all here in the barn," Thomas said, obviously not the least bit delighted.

"Father Coghlan is visiting. Mother asked us to come help you and Joseph," Mary explained.

Joseph was now yelling at Clio.

Ethel, Nan, and I laughed. Mary silenced us with a look.

"What does he want?" Thomas complained.

But he already knew. We all did. Our father had invited the

well-known atheist Mr. Robert Ingersoll to speak in Corning next week, and the priest was here to stop it.

It seemed Father Coghlan had put up with Father's spouting about socialism and a single tax, along with his constant talk about the misery of the working people (whose suffering, my father never failed to mention, the old priest's God never relieved), but to host a heathen might be going too far. It was no secret that if Father Coghlan had his way, the entire Higgins clan would be dunked in holy water—and just like those diapers drying on the line, all of us Higginses would be lined up in a pew for Mass each Sunday. But I thought he would accept our mother putting an end to my father's latest adventure.

She wouldn't.

My mother had ten children, not a one of us baptized. Father wouldn't hear of it. Although she'd been brought up in the faith and still firmly believed in it, she'd married a freethinker, an atheist, a socialist, a proud member of the Knights of Labor. Nothing, not even my mother's iron will, would change this.

I had often tried to imagine the days of my mother and father's courtship. When my father was jolly, he was an easy man to love. Big, with a loud Irish brogue and a mighty head of long red hair, he could talk and laugh and drink more than anyone I'd ever known. My only guess was that my quiet mother fell in love and never looked back. Or, at least, we never saw her look back. She was my father's wife, and Thomas, as well as Mary, Joseph, Nan, John, and I knew she would side with Michael Higgins over Father Coghlan and his Catholic church any day of the week, including Sunday. Including *this* Sunday. And wasn't this what the church asked of her?

All the Irishmen in this town referred to their wives as their ribs because when women married, they were being returned to the body of man. As unpleasant as it sounded, being even the tiniest of piggy toes of any of the rough and dirty men of Corning, would Father Coghlan have my mother go against her own body?

Joseph appeared with a howling Clio in his arms. He took one look at us all, and his anger turned to concern.

"Father Coghlan is here," Mary informed him.

Joseph nodded as he dumped Clio in Mary's lap. "Hush," she told him. He listened. Everyone listened to Mary. Even Clio.

Joseph removed his hat and wiped the sweat from his face. Sighing, he slumped onto the hay.

"Mary?" Ethel asked.

"No," Mary said.

And now Ethel sighed.

We sat and watched the dark close in around us, listening to the chirping crickets and to Richard gurgling in his sleep. John fell asleep too. None of us had anything to say. But I couldn't help wondering what we were each thinking.

Did Mary wish Father would behave? I think Joseph did. Joseph behaved. John, too. Thomas didn't, so he wasn't allowed to be wishing this for Father. Although Thomas misbehaved using his fists, which strangely didn't seem to carry the same harsh consequences as not behaving using words.

Nan. What did Nan wish?

I think Nan wished what I wished, that the world could be big enough for both Father and the Catholic church. That those who wanted to be heaved into a washtub of holy water could do so, and those who didn't would be left alone. She wished workers were paid fairly. She wished the hill of Corning shared a little of the air and sunshine with the flats. She wished that she and I and

Mother and Mary could vote. She wished she could be a writer. Like father, she loved words. She just wrote hers down.

I guess I wished the world were completely different, and Father would behave because he'd have no reason not to? And then the priest wouldn't be in there making my mother . . . *more miserable than she already was.*

I jumped up from the hay. "I'm going back in there."

"Sit," Mary said.

And now I sighed, too . . . taking my seat back on the hay.

I pictured my mother sitting across the marble-topped table from the priest, listening to him speak. Because surely, she was doing just this, sitting quietly, listening. And then the most curious thought crept into my head . . . I wondered what my mother wished?

"Father will be home soon," Joseph said, interrupting my thoughts. It was his way of saying the priest would be gone soon, and this long wait, trying all our nerves, would be over because we all understood the position our mother was in. A position there was no good way out of.

"I want Mother," Ethel whined.

She always wanted Mother. And she always seemed to get her.

"If you're going to behave like a baby, go roll in the pig shit with them," Thomas snapped. I sometimes appreciated my brother.

My little sister wanted to cry, but before she could, we heard the priest's loud voice.

Joseph tossed aside the rake he'd been holding. Thomas swiped the hay from his trousers. Nan woke John. And Mary, Ethel, and I headed for the babies.

We shuffled from the barn, each Higgins wishing Father Coghlan a pleasant evening as we passed him, except for me . . . and Ethel, but mine was in protest. Ethel just didn't have any manners.

We filed into the house past my mother standing in the doorway. She was struggling to hold back her cough. As soon as the door closed, she gripped the doorframe and hacked and hacked and hacked, like every word the priest had stuffed into her needed to be purged from her body. None of us moved. Not even Clio.

Once she had expelled the long, hard conversation, the house sprang back to life around her. No one spoke, but the knock of knife on wood and the clink of plate meeting plate soothed me, and I placed Richard down in his crib and picked up the pail to empty the dirty wash basin from the boys, but then stopped. Instead, I grabbed a clean rag from the rag box, found the soap, and last, grabbed Clio.

I felt my mother's approval just as surely as I heard Clio's screeches ringing in my ears. A cold bath was no fun, but newly acquired pig shit was actually easier to remove than a week's worth of old mud. I had Henry almost finished by the time Father walked in.

"Happy Sunday," he declared as he entered. And it was as if nothing had ever happened.

"Happy Sunday," my mother repeated.

I looked up from Henry's soapy head and caught her eye. It might be Sunday, but my mother wasn't happy.

Satan Visits

"You worry too much, Anne," my father said, waving away my mother's concern. "You will see. Mr. Ingersoll will astound everyone."

But *everyone* wasn't going to hear Mr. Ingersoll speak.

My mother wasn't because she was already growing larger with the next baby, a literally built-in excuse for not going anywhere. The boys barely sat through lectures at school, let alone a lecture on a Saturday. Ethel was too young, Mary too needed, and Nan too good hearted to slip out without finishing her chores.

I was going. And I knew enough to keep my saucebox shut about it. Otherwise, I'd be plucked up for a task that would surely keep me from being astounded. My father had been reading Mr. Ingersoll's speeches to me over my mending and I had to say, unlike Mr. Henry George, Mr. Ingersoll was no bore. Also, there would be lunch.

When Father put on his hat, I slinked quietly for the door to make sure that when he left, I left. My mother had moved on to wringing out the laundry. She knew he would do as he wanted. It was what my father did. And what he wanted was to invite Mr. Bob Ingersoll—great orator, freethinker, and infamous atheist—to Corning to speak *inside of Father Coghlan's town hall.*

It was just the two of us, as we knew it would be. The day was one of those early October afternoons when the sky was bluer than my father's eyes, and the cool air seemed to lift us up with each step. My father was even more excited than I was, and I listened as he repeated all his favorite of Ingersoll's ideas on the walk to the train station. *There is no God. There is no place called hell. And women should be able to wear pants.*

The pants idea he added just for me. He knew how much I loved to hear it. Pants! What a dream. Dresses dragged, pants floated. Just like my father's words. And I couldn't wait to meet this man who would let me wear a pair of pants.

I heard him before I saw him. He was loudly saying his good-byes to people on the train. I knew it was him because my father smiled down at me, his eyes telling me to *get ready.*

I stood straighter, hands at my sides, a serious look on my face . . . a pants-wearing look.

A giant man emerged and grabbed my father's entire arm just to shake his hand. His laugh bounced off my chest. He smelled like starched sweat. "Is this Margaret?" he asked.

He put out his large hand so that I might shake it. I'd never shaken anyone's hand before, so when I didn't immediately reach out, he took my hand from my side and waggled my arm, his dark eyes piercing mine from under great bushy eyebrows that reached off his forehead like antlers off a buck. "I hear you're the big bug."

"Yes, sir," I whispered politely. "A very big bug."

The force of his laugh knocked me backward into my father's coat buttons.

The three of us marched down Market Street, the Chemung River glistening in the sunshine between the buildings. My father and Bob—as he'd told my father and me to please call him—never stopped chattering, not even to listen to each other. Bob was to speak at the town hall at two o'clock. But before this . . . there would be lunch. This "big bug" planned on eating big. I knew my father had money in his pocket and my plan was chicken legs, corn fritters, and mashed potatoes.

I did get potatoes, but they weren't mashed. They were rotten.

The first one hit me in the shoulder. The second one hit me in the shin. Then the air was full of rotten everything: beets, tomatoes, apples, and even dried ears of corn. The corn didn't hurt much. But the apples did. Surprisingly, so did the beets.

My father howled at our attackers to knock it off. Not only did they not listen, they threw more, and with increased vigor, all while dodging at us and shrieking from contorted, angry faces.

Cold spit dripped down my neck and a tomato squished inside one of my boots. I wrapped my arms around my head and tried to move forward down the road, but it was obvious we weren't going to make it to the town hall. My father tucked me under his arm, and the three of us retreated back toward the train station. The distance lessened the amount of rotten food pelting us, and for the first time I heard their terrible words.

"Return to hell!"

"Get thee back, Satan!"

"Witchery!"

"Infidel!"

"Devils!"

Once we were safely back at the station, my father—his face as red as his hair—threatened to return to town and take on the entire tomato-throwing troupe. But a second, smaller crowd at the station convinced him not to, along with Mr. Bob Ingersoll.

"Let them be. Remember, Michael," he said, "anger blows out the lamp of the mind."

Someone suggested that we wash up in the station, and that Bob give his speech over on the other side of the railroad tracks. It was decided. As we crossed the tracks, I said a silent farewell to my mashed potatoes . . . and the sweet butter I had been planning on drowning them in, since Mary wasn't going to be there to stop me.

But once Bob began to speak, I forgot about my empty stomach. Like my father, Bob spoke with powerful excitement about freedom, education, and equality. For everyone. Black, white . . . even women. And like my father, he did not believe in God.

"What kind of god drowns his own children?" Bob asked.

I decided I liked Bob. Listening to him, I forgot all about my back bruised by beets, and the anger-twisted faces of the people on Market Street. His words were gentle and kind and welcoming to all. Sitting out in the woods being warmed by a brighter idea of what the world could be, I thought how wrong Father Coghlan was to worry my mother.

When the McGill brothers left their front porch and followed Joseph, Thomas, Nan, and Ethel down Erie Avenue laughing and shouting at their backs, my brothers and sisters didn't know yet about the rotten vegetables and shower of spittle, or that Father and I were sitting on soft pine needles having our ears filled with Bob's preaching on free thought. My brothers' and sisters' thoughts were on laundry. They'd gone to pick up what we Higginses called "hill laundry," which my mother and Mary washed for people who lived on the hill.

But the McGill brothers knew about Bob. As it turned out, all of Corning knew about Bob.

Even so, those McGill boys should not have followed my brothers out of town. They should have known better. Thomas was small, but he made up for it by punching hard.

We all arrived home at the same time. My brothers were covered in blood, my father and I were covered in beet stains. Nan told us what happened with the McGills. I told them what happened with Bob. When I mentioned the part about God drowning his own children, Nan gasped.

"Everyone will hate us," she said.

"I don't care!" I shouted.

"Enough," my mother ordered.

She commanded all of us to get out of our soiled clothes, and then placed Nan and me in charge of washing out the blood and beet stains. "Every speck of it."

"Every speck?"

Her look withered me. There were a lot of specks. There were even entire splotches.

Nan and I scrubbed until our knuckles were sore and our fingers wrinkled by water.

And on Monday morning at school, when Emma walked right by my desk like I was invisible . . . I cared.

March 1, 1899

Thomas stops the wagon in front of the house to let me off before he takes it around through the alley where he'll tie up Tam before heading back to the factory. He hangs the reins and stands, and I see he's actually going to jump out and help me down from the wagon.

I quickly leap off.

I don't need Thomas Higgins helping me out of a wagon. I don't need anyone helping me out of a wagon.

"Very ladylike," he remarks.

"Never my goal," I mutter, grabbing my bag out from the back.

He snaps the reins and drives away. We don't say good-bye.

I stand before 308 East First Street, a sloping white house sandwiched in between two other sloping white houses, all three of which have been made gray by the factory smoke. It seems the same suspendered little boys with dirty knees and rough and tumble little girls in braids run up and down the street as when I left, their faces and clothes also seeming gray. The flats of Corning . . . an entire neighborhood made gray by the belching black smoke of the stacks of Corning Glass Works, which rise up along the Chemung River like giant stalks of some hardy river plant.

Soon I won't notice the smoke anymore. A few days, maybe a week, and this dirty fog will just be how the world looks. And all the gray brooms left out on gray porches, gray diapers flapping on gray laundry lines, and gray faces of those I pass on gray streets will be a mirror of my own gray face.

I spent most of my life pretending I didn't care—about the smoke, about the squalor, about the gray people with no way out of their gray lives. But as I make my way toward the gray wooden steps into the gray sloping little house, the truth is, I care far too much.

Spawn of the Devil

We were now the spawn of the Devil. Every one of us.

Most days being spawn didn't feel too much different than not being spawn. I changed diapers, washed breakfast dishes, hung sheets, and walked the five miles back and forth to school.

School, though, felt a little bit different. Not while I was doing my sums or conjugating Latin verbs, but all the times I wasn't.

Mary said to ignore it. She ignored it. But, of course, no one called Mary a ratbag. Or shoved her into the woodpile when Miss Hayes wasn't watching. Or worst of all, pretended Mary no longer existed . . . and Clara Martin was her new best friend.

And it wasn't just Emma and school. Everyone in the whole town hated us Higginses. Every last one of us. They hated responsible Mary. They hated sweet Nan. They hated Ethel even if she was only a little kid. And they definitely hated my brothers, although admittedly, Thomas Higgins was quite easy to hate.

They hated us because we were spawn. Children of the Devil. The Devil being my father.

My father, who chiseled the angels that topped the graves of the dead, didn't believe in God or the Devil. He believed in the work of men. The men in town believed in their work too, but they believed in God and the Devil more. I believed in my father, unlike all of Corning, where he had chiseled his last angel. No good Catholic—or Protestant—wanted an atheist near the graves of their loved ones.

It might not be pleasant to be spawn, but I was warming up to it. Spawn meant you believed in something. You fought for something. So be it if that made us different. I didn't want to be like everyone else. Especially people like Emma Dyer, who thought Clara Martin was some great pumpkin.

Mary didn't like being spawn, but she would never admit it. She was an expert at everything, even pretending nothing had changed. My brothers let their fists do their talking. Afterward, people might think of them as spawn as they passed by on the street, but following a few shiny blinkers they didn't dare whisper it. Ethel didn't mind it so much because she thought we were being called swans of the Devil, and none of us corrected her. Nan, though, her heart was too soft for the spitting and the shoving. I knew Bob said there was no such place as hell, but there were a few here in Corning I wouldn't mind seeing fall into its fiery pit.

"Why did he do it?" Nan whispered at night. "Why did he invite that man here to speak?" She believed Bob brought the hate.

I wanted to tell her what Bob said, about anger blowing out the lamp. I wanted to tell her that he didn't bring the hate, the hate was already here.

But I was afraid she'd be huffed. And I liked being all together. Me and Nan and Thomas and John and Joseph and all the rest of us, spawn of Satan together. Even if it meant having Father gone, looking for work. Like Bob, he was living his truth, and his truth didn't live in Corning. Hopefully, it lived in Elmira.

My mother waddled out stomach first and plopped another basket of diapers next to my feet. Wiping the sweat from her forehead that came from a morning of stirring boiling diapers with a dolly stick, she cast a long look at my progress. I followed her gaze to my row of diapers on the line, pinned so crooked they looked like old Mr. Keeler's teeth, all skewed and cockeyed.

"Margaret Louise," she sighed, her meaning so plainly clear. *Nothing you do is done well. What more is there to say? You are hopeless.*

Once my mother had returned to her diaper stirring, Nan popped up beside me. "Let me help, Maggie," she said.

Nan whistled and hung while I handed her diapers and pins.

Another Sunday. Another day of chores. Another day in the lives of the spawn. At least on Sundays there was no school, no town, no shoving, or spitting. There was only the hanging of diapers with my fellow spawn. With the sun high and fall breathing out its last fiery breath of reds and oranges, and the earth still remembering the heat of summer warming my bare feet . . . they couldn't touch us. Not here.

Until we heard a long moan. Not a cough, a moan. Another baby.

Babies were never unexpected, and excited me no more than breakfast or dinner. But this baby was coming too soon, and without Father here. And when I pointed these things out to Mary a few moments later, she got all wrathy.

"I wasn't born in the woods to be scared by an owl, Maggie," she said as she set the water boiling.

Nan scurried over and gave me a hug. Sometimes I wished she'd keep her dang sweetness to herself. It only deepened my worry.

"Are you scared?" I asked.

"Absolutely not," she said, before following Mary into my parents' bedroom.

Ethel looked at me. "Is she?"

I shrugged. I didn't want to say that she was. But she was. We all were, because we all should be. Childbirth might be natural, but so was a hurricane.

Mother's water had only just broken, so we could have hours before anything happened. I wandered outside. Thomas and John were in with the chickens.

"What are you doing?" I asked, curling my fingers through the chicken wire fence.

Thomas didn't look up. "What does it look like?"

I sighed. "Are you staying out here because Mother is laboring?" I asked.

"We are out here because it's time to feed the chickens," John said. "And after this, we will be out here because we need to feed the dogs. And then milk the cow."

He gave me a wink. I smiled weakly back at him.

"But the real question," Thomas grumbled, "is why are you out here?"

Joseph was saddling up Tam, probably to fetch the doctor. John saw me noticing.

"Maggie," he said, opening up the gate and handing me the

chicken feed, "Why don't you finish up here with Thomas and then go in and help Mary with Mother."

I picked at the feed until Thomas snatched the pan from my hands. "Go somewhere else and do nothing," he snarled.

I headed back to the house because it's where my feet took me. I heard the coughing before I even opened the door, so I didn't open it. But Ethel did. She was holding Clio on her hip.

"Wash the breakfast dishes with me?" she asked.

"Did we have breakfast?"

My stomach growled. We both glanced over at the empty sink and then back at each other. We did not have breakfast.

My mother groaned behind her bedroom door. Ethel's lips trembled. Clio began to cry.

"Take Henry and Clio to the barn."

"Why?" she complained.

"Because I said," I snapped. It was the right of all older Higginses to snap at younger Higginses.

My mother groaned again, and Ethel grabbed my hand.

"Maggie?"

"She'll be fine," I told her, my face the likeness of one of my father's stone angels, hard and chiseled into a beautifully serene smile. But my words were complete gum—because I certainly did not know if she would be fine. Although I wasn't about to tell Ethel the truth. I wished Father were here.

"Maggie!" Mary called. The pains must be getting closer. This baby might come quick. I was fast becoming Mary's right hand during injury, illness, and deliveries. Unlike Nan, I had no fear of blood and could withstand the howling of pain.

"I'll fetch you when the baby comes, Ethel. Now go."

The baby didn't come quick. After helping to warm the bath

for when the baby arrived and collecting clean rags to catch the blood and fluids, I sat by my mother's side and held her hand.

I liked this part. Sitting by her side. Sometimes I wiped her face with a rag. It was sweaty work, birthing a baby. The only time I didn't enjoy it was when she coughed. Mary stopped what she was doing and stood in place, as if holding still would help my mother catch her breath. It wouldn't, but I understood. I also sat as quiet and still as possible, blurring my eyes while she hacked so I wouldn't see her mouth slack and her neck straining, her face as white as my father's marble, and her red eyebrows tied together in agony. When a pain came in the middle of a coughing fit, she squeezed my hand so tightly I saw dark spots float past my eyes. Then, when the coughing and the pain finally subsided, she laid her head back against the pillow, where it seemed to swallow her. Mary jumped back into action. I continued to hold her hand.

My stomach ached. I was so hungry. It must have been past lunchtime. But no one was talking about food . . . or where Joseph was with the doctor.

I heard Nan and Ethel in the other room. And then Nan came in with Richard in her arms. She laid him at my mother's breast. Like the rest of us, he was hungry and there was little milk in the house—there was little anything in the house. My mother fed one baby while she attempted to deliver another. How much could one body do?

"Maggie," Mary said as if she'd said it a few times and I hadn't been listening. Maybe she had, because she was standing in front of me holding a cup of broth and I didn't remember her leaving the room. "Nan made potato soup."

I wanted to eat more than anything . . . except hold my mother's hand.

"Soon."

Mary nodded. Her approval made me feel strong, stronger than the pull at my stomach as the smell of broth drifted from the cup to my nose.

The sound of Richard's sucking in the warm, dark room carried me off into a dreamy place. A place on the hill where the houses were large and clean and there was space and light and sunshine. Where there was an abundance of chairs and long hallways with flowers. Where wide green lawns spread out beneath gentlemen and ladies playing croquet and drinking cool drinks and nibbling on tiny sandwiches. Piles of tiny sandwiches.

I saw freedom. From cramped rooms. From laboring mothers. From growling stomachs. From fathers off looking for work.

My father's freedom of the mind was only one kind of free. On the hill, they had another kind of free. My father liked to say that in life it was chicken today and feathers tomorrow. But the people on the hill had chicken every day. Chicken every day— what would that be like?

My mother once knew. She didn't speak about it, but she grew up in a big house in New Jersey just like the fine houses on the hill in Corning. But then my father blew through her town, a wild-talking Irishman dreaming of a better world, a different world. Maybe she thought her life would be different if she married him. Maybe she thought she'd be different too. Her parents did not agree, so she left them behind.

I looked around the crowded bedroom of the cabin. This was definitely different, but I wasn't sure it was exactly what my mother planned on. What was I planning on? Being a doctor.

Buying that big house for Henry—my stomach growled—tiny sandwiches. Living on feathers and dreaming of chicken, is this what made us spawn?

The door opened just wide enough for Joseph's head to slip through. He and Mary exchanged a look. The doctor wasn't coming. I knew instantly it was because of Bob. I was glad Nan wasn't in the room.

Mother was squeezing my hand again. Mary rushed to the end of the bed. Richard had rolled off and was sound asleep next to her, not witnessing his mother's hideous pain or the next Higgins as she slipped quietly into the world. Too quietly. I wondered where my wild-talking father was right now. Was he laughing? Drinking? Working?

My mother looked her baby over with heavy-lidded eyes, and then passed out. Mary gently washed the body in the pot of warm water sitting at the end of the bed to ready it for burial. I waited for the afterbirth. Once we finished cleaning up, I slipped over to steal one last look at her . . . reminding myself that a Higgins didn't cry, a Higgins managed.

The baby was a beautiful thing, with long elegant eyebrows and tiny clenched fists. She could never have been spawn since she was so obviously an angel.

Promising

There were days I would love to live over again, like those where I roamed about in the woods with my sisters hunting mushrooms. And then there were days I'd love to skip altogether, like this one—a cold Monday morning with winter biting into fall, school looming with a classroom full of hate, and the only way there was past another tiny grave.

I was not surprised when Ethel refused to get out of bed, using the most fake croaky sick voice I'd ever heard. Although it was a surprise that Mary believed her. Or rather, Mary pretended to believe her, tucking the little liar back into bed and announcing she would also stay home from school.

Mary more or less missed every other school day anyway. No one said a word, least of all my mother. Most of Mary's friends had already left school for marriage or the factory. She was the oldest in the classroom, not much younger than Miss Hayes. But Mary kept up her schooling, because . . . *Mary was so promising.*

This was what Miss Hayes always said.

Promising for what? Teaching more promising girls to teach more promising girls to teach more, and so on. Promising, a present continuous verb. But this tense was temporary, just like, it seemed, Mary's promise.

"May I inquire as to your thoughts," Nan asked, bumping my shoulder as we walked. The sun was building strength and warming the top of my head. It wasn't winter yet.

"You may inquire," I sighed, "but they're gloomy and thus I shall not share them."

"She's dreaming about Walter Kearney," Thomas said. "Don't try to hide it, Maggie."

I swung my books at him. "Like the Devil loves holy water, I am."

"Walter Kearney is in love with you, and women love having men in love with them."

I almost shouted that I wasn't a woman. Then I almost shouted that Walter Kearney was far from a man. Instead I just shrieked, sounding a bit like a red fox caught in one of Joseph's traps.

"Leave her be, Thomas," Nan soothed.

And Thomas did because Nan asked. Why did he never listen to me?

We walked along, everyone returning to their own thoughts. It was just Nan, John, Thomas, and I. Joseph had stayed home to patch the roof. With father still gone, and snow on the way, somebody had to climb up and stop the leaking. It would be nice to sleep without the wind knocking things off our dresser or the rain pattering into buckets. But now because of my brother, my thoughts were stuck on Walter Kearney.

I admit it was easy to see Walter Kearney favored me, since he was the only boy in class who didn't show the sign of the cross every time he came within ten feet of me. I didn't love him, but the truth was, I didn't mind having him love me. It was better than him hating me like everyone else did . . . like Emma did.

It stung every morning when I walked in and she turned away from me. Our friendship had seemed as real as the braid swinging down my back, as real as the boots pinching my toes.

As we approached school, I reminded myself not to look at her when I walked in. But as soon as I walked in, I looked. And like scratching off a scab that hasn't quite healed, fresh blood gushed from my wound as she quickly turned her face toward Clara, laughing at something funny Clara said. Of course, we both knew she was obviously pretending because Clara Martin had never uttered anything funny in all her life.

I slid slowly into my seat next to Nan, telling myself to do anything but look over at Walter Kearney. This, too, I failed at, and when I glanced over at him, I caught him smiling at me. My eyes darted over to Thomas, who was smirking gloriously. I glared at my brother and then opened my Latin. I hated Latin.

I attempted to get lost in conjugating the past tense imperfect of give. *Dabam, dabas, dabat?* I didn't get lost, and instead found myself looking back over at Walter. He was still staring at me.

Where was Miss Hayes? Had this boy nothing to work on?

I attended to my verbs. But not really. What I really did was scratch about like a mouse at my desk until lunch when Miss Hayes released us into a beautiful fall afternoon, a great day to be anywhere but sitting in a bunch of weeds under a sugar maple outside the schoolhouse eating stale cornbread and cold salted potatoes.

John and Thomas didn't ever stick around for lunch. We had

no idea where they went. I guess we'd never been that interested. Although I was glad they were gone when I saw Walter staring at me from the steps of the schoolhouse.

I sighed.

"Emma getting you down?" Nan asked.

"Emma? No. Never. I don't care a bit about her," I lied.

She looked around and spotted Walter. "Oh."

"Yes."

"It's to be expected," she said. "You're of age, Maggie. Of course boys will court."

"Court?" I barked. "What are you talking about? Court! He's just mooning at me. That is it."

"Mooning. Courting. Same thing."

"I want nothing to do with him."

"Then why have you been staring at him all day?"

I jumped from the grass. "Nan!" I hollered. "I have not been."

Her shoulders slumped. "You have."

"Only because of Thomas. He's made Walter like a sore tooth, and I can't keep my tongue from finding him over and over again."

"He's just admiring you."

"I don't want anyone admiring me," I grumbled, plopping back down next to her in the grass.

But this was an even bigger lie than the one I told about Emma. I wanted everyone to admire me . . . my father, my mother, Mary, Emma. Even Walter Kearney.

"Oh my goodness, he's coming over."

Nan was right. He was walking straight for the woodpile.

"Do something, Nan!"

She laughed into her hands.

"Not that!"

She laughed harder.

"Nan, get a hold over yourself," I whispered.

This had the opposite effect on her. Thank the holy heavens Thomas was not witnessing this.

Walter stopped in front of us.

Nan choked.

"She all right?"

"She's deathly ill," I informed him.

Nan choked harder.

"I'm sorry for that," he said.

"Kearney's in love with Satan's witch!" screamed one of the McGills.

"Satan doesn't have witches, he has followers or minions," I shouted back, rolling my eyes. "Get your hellfire terminology correct."

I heard Clara Martin gasp, and looked pointedly at Nan.

"May I return to my profession of love?" Walter Kearney asked.

"Please, d—"

Before I could finish saying "don't," he did.

"Margaret Higgins. I love you. Despite your unfortunate choice in fathers. I think you are beautiful and will make me very happy."

"My choice? Your happiness?" I sputtered. *Did he say beautiful?*

He smiled. As if I'd understood him completely. Which was true, I actually had. And even though he did call me beautiful, I was choosing to be unhappy.

I stood, so that I might look directly into his eyes. It didn't exactly work because I was taller than he was.

He took a step back. I'd thrown him off with my change in position.

"Walter," I began.

Nan cleared her throat. It was a warning. Be kind. To the boy who liked me because I would make him happy. To the boy who just insulted my father.

I was kind.

"Thank you for your profession of love. You are bricky and bold, Walter Kearney, two qualities I admire. However, I must inform you that I do not love you in return, and therefore do not believe you would be able to make me happy. I sure hope this doesn't ruin your day. And that you're able to love again very soon."

"You're turning me down?" he asked. His face crumbling.

"I don't love you. I'm sorry."

And I was, sorry. Really sorry, as I watched his chest heave, his feet shift in the grass, and his eyes glisten over.

"Well . . . I d-don't love you either," he stammered. "I was dared to say it. You're an ugly witch." He crossed himself and then spit on my boot and stormed off.

"Horrible boy!" I shouted at him, dragging my boot in the grass trying to get his sticky gob of phlegm off me. I could hear Clara and Emma laughing over by the schoolhouse steps.

"She's so dramatic," Emma lamented. My old compliment, thrown back at me. I felt the red fox's sad shriek rise in my throat.

"That didn't go so well," Nan said.

I shook my head in agreement. "Thank God Thomas didn't see it."

"Oh, I saw it," said Thomas as he and John came from behind us. "Funniest thing I ever saw."

"Don't," Nan told him.

Thomas held out his hand. It had two peppermints in it. "One for each of Satan's minions."

"I guess you're not marrying Walter Kearney, Maggie." John grinned. "Maybe he'll ask Nan next."

"Marry?" I grunted. "Nan and I are never marrying anyone. I'm going to be a doctor, and Nan is going to be a writer."

As soon as the words left my mouth, I wished I hadn't said them. Nan and I might say it all the time. But we only said it when it was the two of us. We didn't say it out in the general world. Not that Thomas and John were the world, but at the moment—in this moment—they felt like they were. And maybe they were, really. The world kept growing larger, and in comparison, I grew smaller.

Miss Hayes rang her bell.

"All girls get married, Maggie," John said, swinging the hair from his eyes. It was as if he was saying we all die, which we do, but first I wanted to live. It wasn't that falling in love sounded fatal, it was what followed. I wasn't ready to be someone's rib yet—I'd barely used my own.

Miss Hayes rang her bell harder.

"Or teach." He shrugged, glancing over at Miss Hayes.

We walked toward the schoolhouse. Nan and I lagged a few steps behind, like we didn't want to be too close to them right now. Which, we didn't. I wanted to apologize to Nan, but I wasn't sure for what. I took a closer look at Miss Hayes as I passed her on my way inside. Could I be her? I glanced around the classroom. It was better than death, I guess.

Once we returned to our studies, there were snickers and snorts making their way round the room behind Miss Hayes's back. I knew I was at the center of them. I didn't dare look over at Walter now. Strangely, this made my heart even heavier. Walter was a dirty dog, but still, I liked it better when he was a dirty dog who loved me. And thought I was beautiful.

Miss Hayes had us open our history books. We were reading about the beginnings of the Roman Empire. It felt as if I'd read this a hundred times. Miss Hayes, sensing my disinterest, called on me to stand and answer questions.

"What was the informal alliance called between Octavian, Mark-Antony, and Lepidus?" she asked.

"The Second Triumvirate."

"Who was the second emperor of the Roman Empire?"

"Tiberius."

I could see she was pleased.

"What was the imperial title granted to Augustus?"

"Princeps."

The class seethed with anger at all my correct answers. I could feel them, like snakes hissing and slithering over one another, hoping I would fall into their pit. But I wouldn't. Because I knew the answers. Anyone could know them. You just needed to read the material. I absently rubbed the protuberances behind my ear.

"How long did Augustus reign?" asked Miss Hayes.

"Forty years."

"What were his last words?"

I loved Augustus's dying words, and I couldn't help giving them a dramatic air. "Have I played the part well? If so, applaud while I exit."

Miss Hayes applauded.

"You may sit now, Margaret." She beamed. "Thank you."

I sat, pleased with myself. Not caring one single red-eyed bean that they all hated me . . . they all hated us. Glad even that Walter Kearney no longer loved me.

Nan reached out and squeezed my arm. I knew she agreed with everything I was feeling right now. Not all women got married or become teachers. Because she would be a writer and I would be a doctor. And we would both leave this town in triumph, taking Mary with us. And maybe Ethel, if she pulled herself together.

We opened up our geography books. Miss Hayes made her way through the desks toward me. I could see she couldn't wait to whisper in my ear how wonderful I was. And I couldn't wait to hear it.

"Margaret Higgins." She smiled. "You show so much promise."

There was a whoosh of air as my triumph rushed from the room. I wanted to reach out and grab Nan for support, but Emma was watching. Walter was watching. Everyone was watching.

"Want to mushroom hunt on the way home?" I asked my sister, wearing the most fake smile my lips had ever made.

Snow Angel

Nan and I began hunting mushrooms every afternoon following school. We didn't speak—we just searched. And when we discovered the most wonderful patch of blewits a mile south of our cabin, we actually hugged each other under the oak trees. We might not be able to find our way in the classroom, in Corning, or in life, but we could find fungi. When we arrived home with our third full bucket in a week, my mother actually laughed aloud.

Mary used the mushrooms to make gravy. She rendered down pork fat, onions, and any other manner of things we had in the house. Thomas couldn't stop complaining about the never-ending stench of mushroom gravy, which added considerably to the pleasure of the whole experience. I admit it smelled worse than an outhouse baking in a late August afternoon, but the gravy tasted delicious. And any odor that annoyed my brother was an odor I'd deal with.

My father arrived home one afternoon while Nan and I were out hunting. Later that evening when we returned with a bucket brimming with hen-of-the-woods, all he said in way of greeting was, "Mushrooms."

But my mother whisked the bucket out of my hands with a smile. "They'll be delicious tomorrow morning with eggs." Somehow, she knew how important these mushrooms were to us.

During our third week of mushroom gathering, a white flake floated past my face as I leaned over a dead tree trunk covered in oyster mushrooms. A few yards away, I heard Nan exclaim sadly. She'd seen it too. There were three solid inches of snow on the ground by the time we reached our yard with what would most likely be our last batch of mushrooms for quite a while.

Later that night, when Mrs. O'Donnell blew into the house in a swirl of snow hunched over her newest screeching baby, all I wanted to do was run out into the woods and burrow deeply into the earth and nestle in next to the mushrooms. Instead, I stayed planted in my usual spot next to Ethel, in front of a sink piled high with dirty dinner dishes.

"He threw him out!" Mrs. O'Donnell shouted over the baby's cries. "He threw him out!"

My father was the first to respond. He put down his poetry, got out of the chair he'd been sitting in since he returned from Elmira jobless last week, and closed the front door.

Mrs. O'Donnell's eyes were wild in her red and dirty face. She wasn't speaking or behaving sensibly as she paced and tossed her head, shivering from the cold. "He threw him out!" she repeated.

My mother rushed toward her, but Mrs. O'Donnell backed away, clutching her baby.

"Eleanor," my mother said soothingly. "Eleanor, come sit."

She pulled out a chair and reached politely for Mrs. O'Donnell's arm. But Mrs. O'Donnell wouldn't sit.

"Let her carry on if she likes," Father said, returning to his chair and his book. "It's a free country."

Mother ignored him, but I felt her allowing his words to hang in the air, along with her silent response. *It is a free country, and the people of Corning have freely chosen not to commission their angels from the Devil.* My father hadn't worked since Bob came to town.

Mrs. O'Donnell didn't seem to notice my mother or my father. Neither did her screaming infant. But the commotion brought every single one of my brothers and sisters scrambling into the room. Anything louder than a houseful of Higginses was a wonder in itself, and we behaved like nocturnal animals, watching silently from every dark corner of the house.

Speaking in a hushed tone, Mother tried to reach through Mrs. O'Donnell's frenzy and pull her out. But the baby kept screeching and Mrs. O'Donnell kept repeating herself over and over. "He threw him out. He threw him out." And before we knew it, our own little Richard and Henry were joining in, creating a chorus of screaming babies. I thought back to that day in Emma's room with her dolls. *Use your imagination,* she'd said. Of course, now Emma refused to say anything to me. I wished eighteen babies on Emma Dyer.

The trio of howlers quickly wore down my father's patience. He stepped in front of my mother and confronted poor Mrs. O'Donnell.

"What is it, woman? What's happened?"

Stunned into silence, Mrs. O'Donnell sniffed in, swallowing a face full of tears. But though he might have silenced Mrs.

O'Donnell, my father had no effect on the squawking babies. That job belonged to Mary and Nan, who soothed Richard and Henry using the tried and true method of a bit of honey on their thumbs. This left only Mrs. O'Donnell's howling infant, its cries seeping into every crowded corner of our house.

One after another after another, they rolled in, shrill and high, like a string of misery held together by moments of silence so slight, there was no recovery.

Toss whined and pawed at the door. My father opened it and the dog fled, barking into the night. When he shut the door, the barking was instantly muffled . . . and we understood. Mr. O'Donnell threw his child out. Into the night. Into the snow.

My mother reached for the baby again, and this time Mrs. O'Donnell let it go, as if she might be done with it for good. Mother laid it on the marble-topped table and peeled the wet shawl away.

Not a Higgins moved, or breathed, or gasped. We just stared. The baby was red. Raw. Covered in pustules. His cheeks and chest screeched louder than his mouth ever could. Eczema.

"Oh, you poor little angel," my mother cooed, and I wondered if she was thinking of her own little angel, buried out with the others under the snow.

You didn't need much medical knowledge to know there was absolutely nothing to be done for this baby but to keep his skin dry until the rash subsided—which could be weeks. I grabbed the softest piece of mending in the basket and brought it to my mother. She squeezed my hand as she took the clean linen pillowcase from me, my fingers vibrating from her warm touch. She then gently wrapped the sad screeching creature and rocked him in her arms, and for a moment, it felt as though it was me she was rocking so warm and close.

Father grabbed his coat and headed to the door. "Margaret?" he called. "Let's have us a walk."

For the first time in my life I didn't leap for my coat and make for the door. I didn't follow him. Something held me in place. And it wasn't my mother's touch. It was anger. I was angry. For the loss of Emma's friendship, for the tiny little sister I'd never know, for snapping at this baby and his mother. I was even angry at him for not appreciating our mushrooms.

"Suit yourself," he said, grabbing his whiskey and slamming the door behind him.

The baby screamed. Poor Mrs. O'Donnell slumped into a chair. Mary put on the kettle. My mother rocked the infant. The rest of us returned to our chores. All of us enduring the torment, which we now knew was nothing like that being suffered by the baby in my mother's arms.

As I scrubbed a burnt saucepan, a picture of Mr. O'Donnell blew into my head like his wife had blown into our house. All the hundreds of shift changes at the factory. All the long walks home through the dark. Bent and heavy and finally home, he opens his front door and he shuts himself inside. With a wave of noisy children. With the empty coal bin. With the unwashed breakfast dishes. With the piles of ironing. With his sickly wife throwing together a thin dinner. With this screeching baby. And for a moment, I felt for him, old and ugly Mr. O'Donnell.

But then I imagined him opening his front door, tossing his baby out into the cold, and slamming it shut, just as my father had slammed his own front door shut a few moments ago. There were no doors between Mrs. O'Donnell and her baby. And none between my mother and hers. My father spoke so often of freedom, and tonight, like Mr. O'Donnell, he was somewhere out there, free. Liberty might be a lady, but I'm not sure I ever met a lady who was free.

Although halfway through the dishes, the heat of my anger cooled along with the dirty water in the dry sink, and I wished I'd gone. I'd grown used to being a disappointment to one parent, but I wasn't sure I could live with being a disappointment to both.

One Less Higgins

Babies died. All the time.

Sometimes they died before they were born, their impression so small we only noticed them missing when we didn't see my mother growing larger. Sometimes they died right after, like our last tiny Higgins. They arrived in the world too soon, never taking a single breath. We washed them. We buried them.

Of course I thought it was sad. But I won't lie, it was also a little bit of a relief. One less body to clothe. One less mouth to feed. One less worry in a house crowded with worry.

Babies died all the time. But when they died on you after a year or two . . . or like Henry, after four, it was different. He was really there. And now he was really gone.

Having someone gone should make you feel empty, but it didn't. It filled you up. My stomach was full even though I hadn't eaten. My head was full even though I had no thoughts. Every inch of me was full, so much so that my feet dragged along the ground.

Last week, the first truly cold gale of winter blew in and he took to fever. My father heated the croup kettle until it boiled and I carried it steaming to Henry's bed, where it rose the blanket like a covered wagon above his sick little body. The next morning, when we knew it wasn't working, Joseph took off on Tam to beg for the doctor. But it was too late. By midmorning, Mary and Nan were laying him out on my parent's bed.

I meant to help, but they were done before I could get there. The door seemed so far away.

Everything seemed so far away. The space in the house no longer taken up by his chubby little body was as large as the winter's night sky, yet my knees knocked into every chair and table as I wandered through.

Henry. It had been four days. One day for each of the years he was ours.

"Where are you?" my mother cried out at night.

We laid in bed and listened with our eyes closed. She was worried about him. She couldn't remember his face. She wondered if he ever existed. She thought she made him up.

I wished I couldn't hear it. Our mother crying. Our father talking. He quoted poetry and philosophy to her. She cried harder. My father's big ideas didn't sound as big in the dark.

Mother begged to know if her son was with God. Henry wasn't baptized. But Father didn't believe in God. Not even for her. Not even in the blackest hour of the night.

We listened until we heard her sobs turn into gulps and fade into silence. And I was left to imagine that house I was to buy for us, the bedroom that would have been his very own, and the big featherbed . . . just for Henry and no one else.

* * *

The sweet tang of whiskey made me open my eyes. I was a little surprised at first because I thought I was still awake. Father motioned for me to be quiet and hurry.

Slipping out from under Ethel's leg, I slid off the bed. The floor was so cold it felt wet. Nan turned in her sleep. I froze in place, waiting for her snores to settle, and then I scampered out of the room, avoiding all the known squeaky floorboards.

I didn't bother to change out of my nightclothes, but instead stuck my bare feet into Mary's boots, climbed inside one of the boy's jackets, and followed him outside.

"I need your help, Margaret."

He took off for the barn with me at his heels. I hadn't seen him move like this, with clear-eyed purpose, for weeks. He'd either been off looking for work or camped in his chair mumbling into a book. Whatever he needed me to do, he knew I'd do it.

The night was black and the dew slowed my steps, but I could picture the way in my head just as easily as I could picture the knots in the wallboards across from the seat in the necessary. I looked back at the windows behind me. They were dark and empty.

Once inside the barn, my father lit a candle and handed it to me. He didn't explain anything, but began to collect his tools, along with a couple of bags of plaster. He nodded at the wheelbarrow.

We hobbled toward town along the dark road. He carried the candle, the tools, and the plaster. I glided the wheelbarrow through dips in the road that turned into muddy rain puddles in the spring, and over jutting rocks that stung my bare toes in summer. I realized he was holding on to everything until we were a safe distance from the house so the sound of the tools bouncing at the bottom of the wheelbarrow wouldn't wake anyone. I didn't ask where we were going. Or what we were doing.

Something rustled under the cold dry leaves next to the road. I tried not to flinch, although my heart beat a little faster. I walked this road every single day of my life, but it was different at night . . . the woods were more awake, and it felt as if my father and I were on parade with a thousand eyes watching us from the shadows.

Finally, Father put his tools and plaster into the wheelbarrow and took over, handing me the candle. I focused on my new job as seriously as I did the previous one, holding the candle out so the light hit the ground in front of the wheelbarrow. The wax dripped, and I had to be careful it didn't hit Mary's boots.

"We're going to the cemetery," he said.

I stumbled, a splash of wax burning the soft skin between my thumb and finger.

"The cemetery?" I repeated in a whisper, although no one could hear us out here. We were half a mile from the house. Not even the loud metal shovel clanging against the floor of the wheelbarrow was in danger of waking anyone. My eyes couldn't help glancing down at it, and I quickly looked away.

"You'll stand guard. Alert me if anyone comes."

I nodded in the dark. I had no voice to say, "Yes, Father." Or "I understand, Father." But I did understand . . . didn't I? He used to work in the cemetery, before he became the Devil. It had been months since I'd seen him chip away at a block of marble. But maybe there was a commission? Maybe this was a job?

The soft trill of a screech owl reminded me of the hour, and I couldn't help it, I glanced down at the shovel again. And the plaster. He saw me do it.

"She needs this." His words came out of his mouth like a soft puff of air.

I now understood exactly what he meant to do and I clutched at the candle while my bare feet sweated inside Mary's boots. I walked straight on, never taking my eyes from the puddle of light bobbing on the road in front of me. All I saw was the light. All I wanted to think about was the light.

We naturally slowed as we approached the cemetery. My father stopped the wheelbarrow and pulled the tools from it. I blew out the candle and took the handles of the wheelbarrow. We headed toward the entrance in complete silence.

Outside the iron gates, he stopped and dumped the tools onto the grass. Pulling out his whiskey, he looked around to be sure we were alone and then took a long swim in the bottle. Plugging it, he returned it to his trousers, pushed the wheelbarrow under a naked forsythia bush, and picked up his tools and plaster.

"Stay here," he said. "Only come in if you see or hear someone."

I didn't want to stay, but I didn't want to go. I didn't want him to go either. I wished I was home. I wished I was in my bed with Ethel's cold feet against the back of my knees and Nan's snores buzzing in my ears. I wished that shovel my father had slung over his shoulder was hanging on its rusty nail by the broken window of the barn. I really wished he hadn't brought the plaster. I watched him disappear between the graves and into the dark.

It felt colder the instant he was gone. I wandered back and forth peering off into the dark down Mill Street, dreading the thought of seeing someone, yet at the same time aching to see someone, anyone that might put a stop to this.

The *chssst* of the shovel slicing through earth made me jump, and I grabbed hold of the frigid bars of the iron fence. Yesterday was Saturday. That made today Sunday. Did Father know this? Did it matter? I looked up. The night sky was full of stars. Some looked close enough to touch. Could God really be up there somewhere? My father said no. My mother never said, but I knew she believed it. She believed it all.

The shovel struck wood with a thump. I was shivering so hard I had to hold my lips closed so my teeth didn't chatter too loudly. He knew what he was doing. He knew. It was all right.

Then came a crack of wood.

Henry.

My hands slid down the cold bars and my knees sunk into the wet ground. I let my face fall against the fence, the cold iron cooling each hot cheek.

He chose me. To be out here with him. To push the wheelbarrow. To hold the candle. To stand by while he dug up my little brother's grave.

Not Nan, or Joseph, or Thomas, or Ethel. He chose me.

But why?

Because they wouldn't do it. And I would. I was doing it. He and I . . . together, disturbing sweet, round little Henry.

We should not be able to touch you, my lovely, lovely boy, because you are gone—somewhere wonderful, I hope. I hope so much. But I don't want to think where you've gone.

To the earth? To the worms?

It was wrong, this digging. Father was wrong to do this thing. He was wrong to choose me. And if he thought I was like him, he was wrong about that, too. Because I was not like him. I was not.

Oh how I wished another cold gale would blow through this town and take me away with it.

"Margaret!" he called out in a hushed tone.

I rose from the wet grass as if I'd been dreaming and stumbled toward him.

We headed home. He pushed the wheelbarrow. I held the candle. In its light glowed the white plaster likeness of my dead brother's head, one fine strand of red hair fluttering in the night breeze.

"We'll come back tomorrow. I'll need a second cast to complete the mold."

My feet dragged along the road as I tried to keep up. *I will not return with him tomorrow. I will never do another thing he asks of me. Never.*

March 1, 1899

My father called me home, and here I am.

Home.

At first everything seems foreign: the size of things, the colors, even the smells. But slowly, slowly it all melts into the familiar. The marble-topped table, the warm tang of burning coal, even the ache of seeing my mother's sleeping body barely a wrinkle under the blanket—the shock of seeing this wasted woman gradually transforming into what my mother always looks like sick.

"I need to get back to work," Mary whispers.

I nod. But I don't move from the bedside.

Mary touches my elbow, and we shuffle quietly out of the bedroom, closing the door so Arlington, our youngest Higgins, doesn't wake her.

"I never know what time Thomas, Joe, and Father will get home from their shifts," Mary says. She talks on, about Ethel, the boys, the house, but I'm not listening. I'm busy choking on the crushing weight of shame, of disappointment. That I ever thought I'd be more than this. That I'd do more than this.

"Maggie?"

When I meet my sister's eyes, she sighs. The small breath gives me permission to leap upon her in an enormous hug. "Oh, Maggie," she says, pretending she thinks I'm being absurd, like this is a little too much for the occasion. Still, she hugs me back, feeling as solid as ever. I hold on to Mary, tighter. It's time to let her go, but I can't.

"I'm hungry!" Arlington shouts, and I finally release my sister. Feeling just as untethered as I did before I grabbed her.

"You'll wait until dinner, Arly," Mary informs him.

Dinner. That would be mine to make. Visions of the competent and quick hands of Mary and my mother pass through my mind. I do not have those hands.

Mary walks to the front door and I follow at her heels as I've done all my life. She doesn't ask me if I'm all right because it's not a question that matters. Dinner, diapers, laundry . . . birds needing plucking, fish needing scaling, potatoes needing peeling, there are ash pans to empty, beds to make, and floors to scrub. These are the things that matter. They've just never mattered to me.

She stops at the door. "Oh, I forgot," she says, even though I know my sister well enough to know she's never forgotten a thing in her life. "Father Coghlan visits after Mass every Sunday."

She turns to leave, hoping to close the door behind her after dropping this bit of information, but I don't hold my tongue.

"To drink too much whiskey with Father?"

"To visit her," she answers. Her back to me.

"And this is allowed?" I ask.

She doesn't face me. "Things change, Maggie."

"Not Father, Mary. He doesn't change."

Mary turns around and looks deeply into my eyes. "I put the cabbage in to salt and trimmed the pork joints. How do you think you'll cook the potatoes?"

"The potatoes?"

"Boil them, tonight. They'll be fine with the pork that way."

"All right, I'll boil them."

Now it is her turn to nod, which she does, right before she leaves me. With no last embrace. No long look back. No final words of kindness. All which Mary knows will only serve to break me down instead of propelling me toward the potatoes, where I belong.

Redemption

"Why can't we sit up with Mary?" Ethel whined. "I bet it's warmer up there."

"Suffering is a way of participating in the passion of Christ," I snapped. "Aren't you even listening to the homily?"

We were sitting side by side in Saint Mary Mother of Mercy, a place I never thought I'd find myself, but now felt as though I completely belonged, because everyone belonged. Everyone but my father.

Father Coghlan moved back and forth twenty pews in front of us, swinging a smoking incense ball on a long chain and speaking in Latin. Directly in front of the swinging ball sat the rich of Corning, their names etched in fancy script on brass plates nailed to the side of the pews where they perched on red cloth cushions covering the long, hard benches. Mary sat up front with the Abbotts. She'd begun working for them as a maid after school and on weekends—the Abbotts overlooking the fact she was a Higgins because she could cook. Mary said we needed the money, and we did. But I also thought it was a way to avoid Henry's memory, which lived in every corner of our tiny house.

It had been four months. Four months of Sundays spent here, in the back pew.

But I didn't mind sitting here because I didn't especially like being close to the empty-eyed white marble cherubs flying high over the sanctuary, reminding me of the lifeless cast of my dead brother's head, which was covered by a cloth in my parent's bedroom.

I glanced to my left and was comforted by the statue of the Virgin Mary smiling down at me, her hands praying and a light shining around her head. This statue I liked. This statue I tried to sit next to.

"Maggie?" Ethel whispered.

"Shush," I told her.

"Do you think there'll be oranges?" she continued.

I kept my attention on the Mass, ignoring her, because following the service there were always oranges. It was the only reason she came with me. I promised her oranges—hers and mine. I was here to feel the power of God. I was here to take in all the light this religion had to offer. I was here for redemption. Ethel was here for the oranges.

I sat up straighter and listened.

> "Pater noster, qui es in caelis,
> sanctificetur nomen tuum;
> adveniat regnum tuum;
> fiat voluntas tua,
> sicut in caelo et in terra."

I recognized the words. My stomach growled.

Ethel turned to me with happy, opened eyes. "The bread is coming," she whispered.

She took a look at my face and quickly turned hers toward the flying cherubs.

Over Christmas, the Abbotts made the suggestion to Mary that we Higginses switch schools and attend St. Mary's. And so my sisters and I started at the Catholic school, were baptized, confirmed our faith, and here we were, on line for Father Coghlan's cold, white fingers to place the body of Christ on the tips of our tongues. My brothers also attended St. Mary's, but they didn't attend Mass. From the look of the crowd here, it seemed only women needed to be devout; men must be redeemed somehow through us.

The old priest was pleased we were here every Sunday. And every Sunday, he asked after our mother. To which I replied, every Sunday, that she was "quite well," whether she was, or was not, well. I don't know why I lied. Or even if it was a lie. I just knew my mother would want it reported this way, and so I did. It seemed not only did women need to be more faithful than men, they also needed to always be well.

This Sunday, Nan had stayed home to help Mother with the house and the boys, as we had a new little Higgins, a fat happy baby named Arlington. Next week it would be Ethel's turn to stay home and help. They switched off each week. I didn't take a turn because I was more pious than they were.

"Well, girls, do you feel the severity of religious discipline beating in your hearts anew this morning?" Father asked when we arrived home.

"Yes, Father," Ethel said, not catching his tone.

"How about you, Margaret?"

I hung my coat next to Ethel's, ignoring him.

He sniffed. "I smell oranges . . . or is that conformity?"

Father had never been against organized religion. He had said a hundred times that many people needed it to keep them on the straight and narrow, while others did not. He believed he was one of those who did not. He also believed his wife and children were those who did not. I didn't know what I believed. I was there to find out. I was a *true* freethinker.

Ethel and I headed upstairs to change out of our church dresses and into our work dresses. Weekends we spent doing the family's laundry, since all weekdays were now filled with hill laundry.

"I'll pin," I told Ethel, taking a basket of wet clothes to the back door.

Outside, our yard was strung up with so many laundry lines it looked like a very large spider had taken up residence. It was a chilly April afternoon, but sunny. The crisp air cleared my mind, and also allowed me to be away from Father.

I'm not conforming. I'm looking. For what everyone else sees. Everyone but him.

The cold bit at my fingers as I pinned wet rag after wet rag onto the line.

There is order in religion. And acceptance.

I picked up another rag, but dropped it when my fingers were too stiff to keep hold of it. A bit of quick rubbing and breathing brought them back to life while I tried not to think about the wrathy faces of the crowd the day Bob Ingersoll came to town.

So . . . maybe not acceptance. But order. And order is not bad.

I carried on with the pinning. I was on my monthly and not feeling well and wished to be done with this.

The door opened behind me.

"Maggie," Ethel said, planting a large basket of bed sheets next to my feet. "Mother says to hang these sheets right away."

"But there's no room."

"Mother says to take our clothes down. The hill sheets need to be dried first."

"But it's the weekend."

"Mother says."

"I'm bleeding! And now I'll have to wear cold, wet rags to school tomorrow while they sleep in warm, dry beds?" I raged, gesturing toward the hill.

Ethel shrugged and then turned around and disappeared back inside.

I looked down at the long lines of rags and diapers I just hung. "Damn it all to hell!"

I reached up and ripped one off the line. The pins popped into the air and vanished into the grass.

Damn any order that has me forever pinning wet things to a laundry line. Damn it! Damn it! Damn it!

And before I knew it, I was ripping everything off the line with pins popping and scattering all over the yard. *The church fathers have freedom. The rich on the hill have freedom. My father has freedom. But the only freedom I'm ever going to have is inside my own head. And they can all get the hell out of it!*

An hour's labor undone in the blink of an eye, I plopped, exhausted, onto the cold grass.

My mother appeared from the house with another basket of

sheets and surveyed the situation. "Handily done," she said, "but can you hang them as fast as you can remove them?"

"That's not going to work. I'm not a child anymore." The irony of my little fit hit me at the same time I realized how true my words were.

She plucked a pin from the grass and began, picking up speed as she hung. I reached out and recovered two pins, clutching them in my hand, and watched her. But then I climbed to my feet and joined in, grabbing a sheet and racing to the other side of the yard.

"We can get it all up," she called, breathlessly, hanging as fast as she could now. "Ours and theirs."

"We can't."

"We can!"

I pinned the sheets and diapers closer. And closer.

She did the same. Both of us knowing it would take all day long for it to dry hung like this.

Ethel came out. She watched us running back and forth from the baskets to the lines. "What are you two doing?"

We didn't answer. We were busy hanging the entire town of Corning's bedsheets on the line in record time for no good reason I could think of.

Ethel jumped in, grabbing a basket.

"I'll hang all the menstrual rags on the chicken fence," she called over her shoulder.

"No!" my mother and I shouted together.

"On the line inside the barn?" she asked.

"Better," huffed my mother.

We were done within an hour. We collected the baskets and then stood and took in our work. Our yard looked like a hurricane had hit it. My mother's cheeks were red and her eyes bright. Her body was not bent over in a coughing fit, but standing straight and strong while she inhaled the fresh spring air, with laundry basket on hip.

"Happy Sunday, Margaret Louise," she said.

Still facing the laundry, she smiled. The first one I'd seen since Henry died. I couldn't stop myself from smiling too.

Damn her for making laundry fun.

Citizens

At first I thought it might be a dream.

Chickens squawking.

Mary in her nightclothes. Sliding out of her bed.

I wiggled away from Ethel, who always slept in the middle. We told her it was because she was safest between us, but truly it was because the middle of the bed was the worst position to occupy, and neither Nan nor I wanted it. Mary's bed was empty because she was tiptoeing out of the room. It was not a dream.

The chatter of the chickens became louder, and I was truly awake. I leaped from bed and followed my sister down the stairs and into my parent's bedroom.

"Mother, someone's in the hen coop," Mary whispered.

My mother did not need to hear this twice.

"Michael, wake up. Michael!"

"What is it?" he asked, still mostly asleep.

My mother was already out of bed, tugging at him. "Some-one's in the hen coop."

"How do you know?"

"Michael, get up!"

Father dragged himself from bed.

Mary ran to the window and peered into the blackness. Again, I was right behind her.

Our breath fogged the rain-speckled glass, and I couldn't see farther than a clump of grass growing next to the sill. But the chickens sure were streaked over something.

My mother lit a lamp as my father stumbled out of the bed-room in his trousers and shirt, fumbling with his cuffs. Not even thieves deserved less than his best. She handed him the lamp and he opened the door, holding the lamp up to the dark night. Mary and I cowered behind him, craning to see. We jumped at the sight of the men in our yard, as if we'd all just now fully woken up. There were two of them, huddled in the dark. Each of their fists was wrapped around a hen's neck, making it difficult for them to unlatch the gate and make a run for it.

"Hey, you there!" my father shouted. "What do you mean by coming to a man's house in the middle of the night and stealing his chickens? What kind of citizens are you?"

Mother pushed us aside. "Michael!" she shrieked. "They're stealing the hens! Go out there and stop them!"

"It's raining."

"Give me that lamp."

My mother snatched the lamp from his hands and ran out into the spring night in her bare feet. The hens laid eggs. Eggs we ate. Every day.

"Drop those chickens!"

At the sound of my mother's shouts, the hounds started in, snarling and barking from their pens. This considerable noise livened up the thieves, and they struggled harder to untangle themselves from the hen coop gate. One of the men dropped his hen. The other tripped over it.

I could feel my brothers and sisters gathering behind me, those that were free from a crib.

"Now then, Anne!" my father shouted. "Let them have one chicken. The boys are most likely just hungry."

This sent my mother into a mighty frenzy.

"NOT A SINGLE HEN! NOT ONE SINGLE HEN!"

The O'Donnells lived nearly three quarters of a mile away, but they surely were sitting bolt upright in their beds at this very moment.

My father threw his hands in the air as if this was all too much. "Come now, citizens," he called out to the men. "Do you see the trouble you're causing here?"

The men saw it, or at least they heard it: My mother screaming. My father shouting at her to return to the house. The dogs barking. The babies crying. And of course, the chickens squawking up a feathery storm.

The men rolled out of the henhouse on top of each other without a chicken in hand. Picking themselves from the wet ground, they lumbered off between the trees and into the dark night while a rogue hen squawked off in the opposite direction behind the barn.

My mother took off after it.

"Anne!" my father called.

We stood in the doorway, a crowd of us now, and stared out into the rain where my mother had disappeared around the side of the barn. The hens settled. A whistle from my father quieted the dogs. The babies kept crying—whistles didn't work on them. None of us moved.

About ten heartbeats later, Mother stomped into sight, chicken in hand, and I realized with a happy pang that I had never doubted her. She splashed through a yard of muddy puddles over to the henhouse, where she opened the gate with ease, tossed in the hen, and latched it shut.

We backed away from the door as she approached, her presence so large and commanding, it needed the entire doorway, doorframe to doorframe, to allow her through.

"To bed, all of you."

In a flash, I was under the warm blanket curled up next to Ethel, the only one of us who was still fast asleep.

Mary had Richard tucked into bed with her. Arlington had stopped crying, too.

But I couldn't sleep. Not even after my frozen feet had warmed. Instead, I watched Mother turn the corner of the barn over and over, her nightgown whipping in the rain and the chicken firmly in her grasp.

I could tell my sisters weren't sleeping either—Nan snored if she was sleeping and Mary cleared her throat if she wasn't—and I wondered if they too were swollen with a strange joy over the memory of our mother striding out from behind the barn.

I fell asleep with excited tears in my eyes.

But I woke later to the coughing. Coughing that didn't stop.

Not for a long time.

Blower Dogs

The school term had only four weeks left in it before summer break, but Joseph said they couldn't wait.

"It's better to go now," he said. "The jobs may not be there in a few weeks."

He didn't add that it was also better now because our mother had been delirious with pneumonia since the night of the chicken thieves and she wouldn't know they'd quit until it was too late. But he didn't have to add this. We all knew it.

Education was everything to my mother, and though Mary might have missed endless amounts of school over the past year, even she still continued to attend. Not anymore. Now four of my mother's children would be leaving school permanently. Joseph, John, and Thomas to the factory and Mary to stay home to care for the house and babies until Nan and I returned in the afternoon, at which time Mary would walk the five miles to the Abbotts to take care of their house and babies—with all the money they made supporting the ever-growing Higgins household.

My father hadn't left my mother's side. He did not take part in this decision.

At first, I also refused to take part . . . by knocking over my chair and marching away from the marble-topped table. But this just made the vote take longer. Mary righted the chair while Thomas hauled me back by my ear. And when I returned to my seat—against my will—Ethel was sitting in Nan's lap and I burned even hotter. Ethel was mine to soothe.

I was the only one to raise my hand against. But then Ethel changed her vote and raised her hand with mine, and I mostly forgave her for seeking comfort from Nan. Although we still lost the vote.

We left in our usual group for school and split up in town. Nan, Ethel, and I headed to St. Mary's; Joseph, John, and Thomas to the factory. The first day was the worst. I could barely watch their backs as they walked down State Street toward the smoke. Ethel was the only one of us who didn't understand.

"Will they meet us later in school?" she asked.

"No, Ethel," I snapped. "They will not meet us later in school."

"Maggie." Nan grimaced.

"Don't grimace at me, Nan. It's time she grew up."

My statement rang with so much truth it stunned Nan into silence. A silence so awful, I snatched Ethel's hand and held it all the way to school.

After about two weeks, it was just those awful first few moments away from them that burned. I counted the steps between us . . . one, two, three . . . to keep my feet walking in my direction as I listened to their voices moving away in their direction. The factory was only a few blocks downhill from school, but it was another world. A world without the possibility of becoming something other than a factory worker. It was an end, not a beginning.

Walking home was better. We'd had the whole day to grow accustomed to their absence. On the way home, Nan and I walked like normal people. And Ethel hummed.

"Stop humming," I told her.

Ethel didn't hear me . . . because she was humming.

"Ethel, cut it out."

She still didn't listen, so I walked up ahead to be away from her. Nan kept up.

"Maggie?" Nan said.

"Hmm?"

"I should really like to be a writer."

"I know."

"Do you think I will be?" she asked.

This she had never done—question it.

"Nan . . ."

She reached out, and with a touch of her fingertips to my sleeve, stopped me from saying another word. She didn't want me to lie. But she also didn't want me to acknowledge the truth . . . that she would be next to leave school.

And then me.

And then little humming Ethel. Who still sometimes sucked her thumb between us at night. Who knew nothing of fiery furnaces and molten glass and blow pipes. Neither did Nan. Nor I.

Of course, we'd *seen* the almighty iron wheel the roughers used to cut the patterns, and the smaller stone wheels dripping with water used by the smoothers. There wasn't anyone in

Corning who hadn't been inside the factory for one reason or another. But we'd never stood all day next to the raging furnace burning as hot as hellfire through which the gaffers remelted their glass at the end of their pipes so they might blow it out into tableware, chemist jars, thermometers, and light bulbs.

Women could never be gaffers, the men who blew the glass. It wasn't allowed. Neither could we be roughers or smoothers or cutters. All those took years to learn, and women were only expected to work until they married and began having children . . . despite any skull protuberances they might or might not have.

My brothers had become "blower dogs," apprentices to the gaffers. They could aspire to blow glass one day. Although how much a gaffer earned depended on how fast Joseph, John, and Thomas could fetch and tote around the heat of the ovens. So, it had better be fast. They arrived home each night dried out like raisins, covered in dirty sweat and shrunken from the heat of the furnaces.

Mary washed their clothes right away so that Mother didn't see . . . so she didn't know. She would, of course, find out, as my father and I took turns nursing her through yet another brush with death. But when she did, there would be nothing to be done but her duty . . . which was to climb out of her sickbed and deal with what she found when she did.

It was what Mary was doing. Her duty. When Mother splashed through her first puddle that rainy night without her shoes, she set up Mary's destiny to step into them. Mary was good at being our mother. She'd been practicing the job for years.

"I think Mary should have liked to have been a theater director," I said.

"That is true," agreed Nan. "And she would have been so

good, don't you think? She knows everything about the theater and she has such moral clarity."

"Moral clarity is definitely a Mary trait." I rolled my eyes and sighed.

Nan gave me a poke with her elbow. But she knew I was playing.

We walked along. I thought of Mary, and what she would be now instead of a theater director. And then Nan—kind and loving Nan, who excelled in writing and languages, and reminded every one of us Higgins how much goodness there was to be found out there in the world. And to be written about.

I stopped still and turned to my sister, whom I loved so very, very much.

"You will be a writer, Nan."

She threw her arms around me. "And you will be a doctor," she whispered into my thick braid.

It was the first time we'd ever said these things to each other without believing them.

Ethel walked by us . . . humming.

Evicted

It's because of the chicken thieves, he said.

We are safer in town, he said.

It's my decision, he said.

But I saw the look on my mother's face when she read the letter. And I watched her take in the old cookstove, the opened front doorway scattered with discarded boots that none of us had worn since summer began, and the sun streaming in through the dirty windows. I saw the look—and I knew. We were being evicted.

It seemed even three blower dogs and a part-time maid didn't make enough money to keep twelve skinny citizens in a run-down cabin . . . and we were soon to be thirteen. My mother, after another near-death experience, was pregnant again.

We had until the first of October to leave, but it was decided we would move out before school began. The morning of the move my father was off looking for a job. But we didn't need his help.

With my mother as foreman, Thomas and Joseph taking care of the marble-topped table, and the rest of us toting the clothes and pots and dishes out to the wagon, we packed up every button and stocking belonging to a Higgins in less than five hours.

I was thankful for the gray sky and the muggy rain. It was like a gift to have something to get puckered over. When the rain picked up, Thomas threw an old blanket over the pile and together we tied it down.

"Damn this weather," he complained.

"I like it," I said, happy to be disagreeing with Thomas on a day like today. It made things feel more normal.

My mother and Ethel climbed into the wagon with Richard and Arlington. The rest of us would walk. Our new home was above my father's shop in town. I had no idea how this would work, but I was sure my mother would figure it out . . . as she did everything else.

The babies settled on Ethel's and Mother's laps, and Joseph gave a tug on Tam. Thomas and Clio walked up ahead of the wagon. But I wasn't ready to go.

"I'll stay behind and help Nan and Mary clean up."

Nan and Mary had been commissioned to clean the cabin for whomever the new renters were. In the next few hours the only home I'd ever known would be cleaner than I'd ever known it.

"No, you won't, Margaret Louise," my mother said. "You'll say good-bye to your sisters and then catch up."

I was stunned. An offer to help in the Higgins household was never turned down.

She noticed my surprise and added, "I need you when we get into town."

I wanted to believe her.

The wagon rolled away.

"Margaret Louise!" she shouted. And as usual, I understood her full meaning. *Do as I've told you to do. Say good-bye and follow us to town. And don't be longer than necessary.*

I watched the wagon for a few moments. Mostly because I was afraid to turn around and see it . . . the emptiness of what once was full.

Too full.

But now I ached for the fullness—hens squawking and dogs barking, flapping laundry and teetering toddlers, the lantern with its broken handle. I didn't want to see it all missing.

Nan's and Mary's muffled voices floated from the house.

I turned around.

The dead grass by the front door looked browner without any buckets or shovels sitting in it. A feather caught my eye as it drifted over the empty henhouse fence. Everything was gone.

I'd spent the last few days packing it up, and all morning hauling it out, so you'd think it shouldn't be a shock. But it wasn't over then. It was now.

Nan came out of the house with a pan of dirty water and dumped it outside the front door. "Maggie," she smiled, clearly startled.

"I wanted to stay behind and help, but Mother said no."

"Mary and I can do it," she said, recovering her composure. "And I'm sure Mother will need you when you get . . ." She stopped, not knowing exactly what to call where we were heading.

"Nan!" Mary hollered.

"I'm outside," Nan responded. Adding, "With Maggie."

Mary popped to the door. "Hey, Maggie. I thought you were going with Mother?" She looked worried.

"She is," Nan told her without taking her eyes from mine. "Mother needs her help once they arrive at the shop."

The empty yard was strange. The quiet was strange. And now Mary and Nan were strange. I needed all this strangeness to stop. I must have looked exactly how I felt because Nan dropped her pan into the grass and hurried over.

"Now, now, Maggie," she said, wrapping her arms around me. "Everything is fine."

Fine. Fine was a bunch of gum. It was what we said to each other when nothing was fine. When fine was a long way off.

I sniffed and pushed Nan away. "May I go in and see it?"

"Don't pile on the agony, Maggie," Nan said.

"Let her see it," said Mary. "It'll give her some peace."

And because Mary said it, I aimed to make it true. I stepped through the cabin door, and the emptiness of the room crawled into my belly. There was nothing but a broom and some buckets and rags. It didn't look a thing like ours. Not like the place where Joseph chased John into the edge of the cookstove and busted open a gash in his head the size of a barn door. Or the place where I held tiny little Ethel on my lap for the very first time. Or the place where Henry was alive. Mary and Nan were scrubbing it all away. And for the first time I realized even the stars at night weren't permanent. Something you'd think my little Henry Higgins would have taught me.

"Say good-bye now, and catch up to the others," Mary instructed.

"Good-bye," I said, because she told me to, and then I walked out fast, not wanting Mary to know that seeing it didn't give me peace.

★ ★ ★

I was tuckered out by the time I caught sight of the wagon—still piled high with our life—standing outside of my father's monument shop. Joseph and Thomas were hauling out the chest that always sat at the foot of my parent's bed.

"There she is," Thomas snorted when he spotted me. "You sure are all-fired lazy, Maggie. Making us do all the work out here in this heat while you drag your feet about town."

I stopped and looked up at him standing in the back of the wagon. It reminded me of another wagon . . . filled with children clamoring for bananas.

"Not going to get all streaked at me?" Thomas asked.

And when I didn't, he told Joseph to hold on, jumped out of the back of the wagon, and walked over to stand in front of me.

"Are you going to hug me?" I asked.

"I didn't want to have to," he replied.

"If you hug me, Thomas Higgins, it means things are much worse than I thought."

He crossed his arms in front of him and laughed. "You are a bad egg, Maggie Higgins."

"I'm about soured on holding the other end of this chest," Joseph growled.

Thomas thumped me on the head and then turned and jumped onto the wagon, getting back to work. It was what my brothers did. Work. Hard. Like my mother. And my sisters.

I pulled my mother's fire irons from under the blanket and placed them by the door to the shop. And then reached in again and yanked out her kettle and blacking brushes, creating a little pile by the door. Though I was sweating and tired, I kept working.

Ethel bounded down the side steps from the room over my father's shop, our new home.

"Let's be a team," I told her. "I'll pile things here and you take them up to Mother."

Ethel loved the idea.

We unpacked like this until it was so dark that I couldn't tell if the wagon was empty, and needed to search the bottom of it with my hands.

"I'll take care of Tam and the wagon," Joseph said. "You go on up."

There was nothing left to keep me, and so I headed up the stairs.

It looked like sheet-cleaning day, as my mother had hung them up to create walls in the single large room. Thomas dragged things about under my mother's direction while she breastfed Arlington, sitting at the marble-topped table lit up with candles. Clio played with Richard next to her in his high chair.

"Come see our room," cried Ethel.

"Wash up for bed, first," Mother said.

I looked around for someplace to wash.

"Basin's on the shelf."

Ethel and I washed our faces and hands, and then wiped up with a clean rag hanging from a nail next to the shelf.

It will be fine. This will be fine. See how she has the rag ready. Everything will be fine.

Ethel took my hand and led me toward a dark corner where our bed was set up . . . without sheets. Mary's bed did not sit next to it.

"Mother?"

"Yes, Margaret Louise?"

"Where is Mary's bed?"

"Mary will be sleeping at the Abbotts."

I swayed in the dark, reaching out for the wooden post of the wall to steady myself.

"And Nan?" I choked.

"Your sisters have taken jobs on the hill."

Her voice was strong, her tone final. I didn't ask anything more, but climbed out of my clothes and into my nightclothes and under the blanket next to Ethel.

"Maggie?" Ethel whimpered.

"Everything is fine," I whispered.

March 1, 1899

I drag a stool over to the large pan filled with potatoes and get to work. By the time the hoard of Higginses arrives home from school and factory, my mother has still not woken up. Joseph greets me with a swat of his hat, Ethel and Richard with a hug, and Clio with a shout of disappointment when he sees I'm the one making dinner. Thomas grunts; he's done his greeting. My father arrives last. He bows deeply before me, and my stomach twists at the recognition of his dramatic gesture. Like father, like daughter. And I'm happy to be forever surrounded by my brothers and sisters . . . better to dilute his presence.

Over a horrible dinner of boiled potatoes and overcooked pork joint—Clio was right to express displeasure—I hear the news. John is working in a mine somewhere out west. Emma has married a man from Utica. "She's as fat as a cookstove with her first," Ethel tells me. Old Mr. Keeler passed away in late

January. And Mrs. O'Donnell gave birth to her fourteenth child last month. We don't speak about my mother's latest loss in the very same month. Always a baby. I've almost never known my mother alone in her own body.

Ethel begins cleaning up the kitchen while I check on my mother. She is still asleep. I've been home for almost four hours and we still haven't met eyes . . . which actually feels like old times.

I pick up the bucket of scraps for the dogs and head to the front door. Richard and Arlington are rolling around on the wood floor knocking into things. My father is in his chair reading, not noticing them batting up against his shins.

"Wash your faces and teeth," I command. "It's time for bed."

Neither of them responds.

"Richard? Arly? Do you hear me?"

Nothing.

"Hey!" shouts Joseph, stamping the mud off his feet in the front hall. "Listen to your sister."

"Yes, Mary," they respond.

"I'm Margaret."

They look up at me from the floor.

"My name is Margaret, God rot it!"

"What?" asks Richard.

I trudge out of the house with my bucket, planning on slamming the door behind me, but when it comes time to yank it closed, I no longer have the energy. . . . I still have so much to do before I can crawl into bed. My bed. Next to Ethel's. At least we each have our own now. Clio, Richard, and Arlington share our old one.

Returning from the dog pen, I meet up with Thomas on the

front flags. He's clean and shaven and wearing a hat.

"Where to?" I ask.

"Out," he says.

"Out," I repeat.

Out. Somewhere. Where he wants. Where he doesn't have to tell me.

"Wait," I tell him. "I'll grab my overcoat."

"What?" he says, just as feckless as his younger brothers a moment ago.

I shake my head in fury.

"Maggie?"

"I wasn't really coming," I tell him. "I was making a point."

"About what?" he asks.

I whip the bucket across the yard at him and storm toward the house.

"You're off your chump, Maggie!"

I don't answer him.

"You missed me, by the way," he snarls.

"You'd have been hit if I'd meant to hit you," I snap back without turning around.

He slams the gate. I slam the front door. I know I need to retrieve that bucket, but I can't bring myself to go after it now. Instead, I snatch up a clean dishrag and join Ethel in front of a stack of dirty dishes.

"Not much changes," she says, handing me a clean, wet pot.

Me, least of all, I think.

Crossing Over

After the day Mary and Nan left for the hill, everything was different. I was different. I realized there were two of me. There was the me who thought before she acted, who worked hard, and who accomplished her tasks.

But there was this other me. A me who was filled with feeling. A me who struck out at Thomas. Snapped at Ethel. A me I couldn't control. This was the me I needed to fight against. This was the me I aimed to stamp out.

During the next six months, I was given more than my share of hard work to practice with since there was only my mother, Ethel, and me to clean the vegetables, to wash the dishes, to hang the laundry, to change the babies. To cook and sweep and mend and all the hundreds of things that needed to be done. Neither Ethel nor I complained, of course, because we got to attend school, while Mary, Nan, Joseph, John, and Thomas paid for our newly rented house on the flats. A house with wooden walls instead of sheets and a real cookstove instead of scalding yourself while stewing meat over the open flame of the hearth in Father's shop. Or rather, Father's old shop.

The shop was gone forever, and my father's independence with it. He worked for the two other stonemasons in Corning now—when he could make himself get up in the morning after drinking whiskey all night, or they didn't throw him out before lunch for arguing with the customers over voting rights. Otherwise he sat in his old chair in our new home while he read and sipped and pretended that nothing had changed, nothing was different.

But I refused to sit by. Or even to be content with working harder. If I was to become this better me, I needed to gain fortitude. So to this end, I began to do the things I feared most. I wandered deep into the woods on mushroom journeys far from any paths. I strutted past the McGill's with every last one of those ratbags standing out on their front porch howling insults at me. I visited Henry's grave alone after dark. When I was able to accomplish these things over and over again without running, without hesitation, without even so much as an extra beat of my heart, I felt the right me growing stronger. But always ahead lay my greatest fear—crossing the narrow, iron span of the Erie Railroad tracks under which the Chemung River raced, deep and fast, far below—*really* far below. If I could cross the bridge, I knew I was truly in control of myself and nothing would ever rattle me again.

Across the Chemung lived the Edders, friends of my father's. Their apple orchard, heavy with white blossoms this time of year, was dazzling. The smell alone made you woozy. But to reach it by the wooden wagon bridge was three miles around. My brothers preferred the shorter route over the high iron span of the railroad bridge. The space between the ties seemed not to hold any terrors for them. Those spaces held considerable terrors for me.

I'd often made the trip across with them, always between Joseph and John . . . never Thomas. I didn't trust Thomas not to pretend to shove me over the edge and have me fall to my death by accident. Just the thought of falling—even while lying safely in my bed—had me grabbing at my bedsheets to steady myself.

But today was the day I'd planned to do this thing. It was actually the fifth Saturday in a row I'd planned to do this thing, I just kept losing my nerve. However, I'd learned the only way to accomplish a thing—a thing you were very afraid of—was to keep attempting it. The first time I headed out to cross the bridge, I turned around at the gate. The second and third times I made it all the way to the bridge, but knew I wouldn't cross before it even came into sight. The fourth time, I stepped out onto the first tie. This morning, who knew? I felt strong.

I started out alone. Strangely, I was often alone these days. I walked the wagon bridge out of town and around past the road that led to our old cabin by the tracks. That life felt as if it had been a hundred years ago, and I wasn't tempted at all to walk the old way to see it.

It was a beautiful morning. The air smelled like green leaves and wet dirt, two smells I loved. For a while, I forgot where I was going and got lost in the breeze and the sun and the chattering birds. My legs carried my body as if it weighed nothing at all, as if everything inside me—my bones, my organs—had vanished. But when the bridge came into sight, my blood began to pump in my temples. I couldn't yet see the river, since it was a dizzying distance below, but the thought of the long, long drop to the water quickened my breath and slowed my steps.

I gathered strength in the familiarity of the sugar maples wagging in the sunshine, the springy soil beneath my feet, and even the rusty bridge standing in front of me.

"Hey, y'all, hey, y'all, hey, y'all!"

It was just Mr. Edder calling his cows to a fresh field, but he startled me near to death. I scanned the trees across the bridge, but couldn't see him or the cows. I looked back from where I'd come. It was only three miles back over the wagon bridge. I should just . . .

"Hey, y'all, hey, y'all, hey, y'all!" Mr. Edder called out again.

I looked back at the train trestle, the midmorning sun making me squint. I'd been here before. Like this. And not crossed. If I did not do this—if I did not cross—I was not who I wanted to be.

With that thought carrying me forward, I stepped onto the first tie. And the next. And the next. And the next, next, next, next, next, next . . . until I froze. My chest ached, my legs were shaking, my breath rasped in my ears. Staring at the weathered wood at my feet, I blurred what flowed far, far down between them. My head threatened to float off my shoulders, abandoning me right here on the bridge.

I took another step, my heart fluttering like a maple seed spinning down from a high branch. I took another. Carefully. Slowly. I watched each of my feet plant themselves onto the next tie.

How far had I gone? Halfway? Was I getting close?

The questions swirled in my head like the river swirling beneath the bridge a hundred feet below. But I dared not look up. There was nothing in the whole world but the next tie, and then the next.

Except . . . for a shiver. Under my foot.

A tiny zinging like a low hum.

The train.

I looked up—not caring about falling because now there was something far worse than falling. I was halfway across. Not nearly close enough. The tracks shook as the whistle blew so loudly it seemed to be coming from inside me. I couldn't see the train because the tracks twisted off into the distance around a hill covered in treetops. But it was coming, and at full chisel.

I turned around and started back. One tie. Two ties.

The tracks visibly shook.

Three ties. Four ties. Five ties.

The train blasted around the hill.

I wouldn't make it. I couldn't make it. This was a mistake. Everything was a mistake. I wanted to take it all back.

The train hit the trestle. My foot wobbled. My arms shot up into the air.

I was falling.

My arm hooked a tie, my jaw cracking into wood. The smell of tar filled my nose as my legs swung out into the air high over the Chemung. The engine crashed toward me. The screech of steel against steel was louder than I could ever scream.

I shut my eyes and hugged the tie with all my might.

Would it slice off my arm and send me spinning down into the river? Would steam pour out and boil me to my bones? Should I let go?

Car after car after car after car crashed over my head. The tie did its best to shake me free. I clung tighter. My arm was not sliced off. Nothing burned me. Hell was dark and loud and long. And still I hung on.

The whistle sounded far off in the distance. My arms were numb against the wood and my shoes had long since spun away, but I continued to dangle in the dark. Until a force lifted me through the ties, ripping my arms from the railroad tie.

"Open your eyes," a man growled.

I didn't open them. I couldn't.

The strong arms shook me, hard. "I said open them eyes, now!"

I obeyed, and was looking into the loose-cheeked, freckled face of Mr. Edder.

"Does your father know where you are?" My thoughts were as numb as my arms, and all I could do was stare at him. "Well, does he?" he barked, his crooked yellow teeth inches from my face, his breath smelling like cooked rice. My chin dropped to my chest.

He let go of my arms, and I saw his hands were trembling. "Go home," he said in a hoarse whisper. Then he turned and walked away across the ties.

I looked one last time at the other side. I shuddered as a thought crept up my spine: I could still do it.

Shaky and weak, but focusing on the sight of the track ahead of me, I took a step and then, without even making a decision, I started to run, listening to the puck, puck, puck of my stockinged feet hitting ties.

Until they hit dirt.

Until I was across!

I collapsed onto the riverbank. I had made it. I had done it. I had never felt more secure, more solid within myself than I did right then. I clutched at the earth, giddy to be lying on it and not down in the river broken to pieces. I would need to do this again. Several times. Maybe several hundred . . . before I could cross it fearlessly. But not today. Today, I'd done it.

I dragged myself from the ground and slapped the dirt and leaves from my skirt, not looking back at the bridge or down into the fast-moving water of the Chemung. In my stockinged feet, I wandered through the apple trees bright with white blossoms, so potent they made me giddy. Every breeze brought a shower of petals. I held out my hand and caught some in my palm and then blew them off into the bright blue sky. When I'd finished sucking in the heavenly scent, I turned toward home, my long braid slapping against my shoulder.

I reached down and untied the ribbon, but my hair stayed tangled in its braid, as if it didn't know how to be unbound. I ran my fingers through the long, red strands, teasing them loose. My hair, liberated, blew about collecting apple blossoms.

The Gloves

A poor girl from Corning would become a poor woman from Corning. This was a truth I'd lived every day of my life. A poor girl from Corning becoming a doctor? It would take strength. Strength that I might not yet have, but I knew how to grow.

My secret successes were mounting. I was slowly learning to control myself. My manners and conduct were impeccable because I had made them so. I dwelt inside a fortress of my own building, a place no insult could penetrate. Nor could anyone else's idea of who I was—or was not—ever again find its way inside. Even Mary and Nan had noticed the changed me, and they'd bought me the most special gift: a pair of beautiful silk gloves.

Creamy white, they hugged each of my fingers and slipped softly up my arms and around my elbows. I would have cherished them whether or not they'd come from Mary and Nan. But I adored them even more because they did.

"Margaret Louise!"

I kept them under my bed in their golden box where I pulled them out to try them on each morning before school, if only for a moment.

"Margaret Louise!"

I admit they were an indulgence. But they were such a lovely indulgence coming from my sisters, who had no money for such folly, but spent it anyway.

"Margaret Louise!"

My mother. Just shouting my name meant so many things. *There are diapers to change. An ashpan to empty. Water to fetch. Chickens to feed.*

I waved good-bye to congenial imaginary people on a charming imaginary city street just to admire my gloves in action one last time before I needed to place them away for the day.

"Margaret Louise!"

"Coming!" I shouted, resisting the urge to shriek it.

The only time she *ever* spoke to me was when she wanted something. Was a single peaceful moment alone with my beautiful gloves too much to ask?

I sighed and then carefully removed finger after finger. Folding one on top of the other, I gently laid them on the silky paper inside their golden box. I replaced the lid, and slid the box under my bed. It was going to be a very long day without them.

After I dumped the ash bucket, I headed out to feed the chickens. On my return trip, I passed my brothers hurrying off to work.

"You left the chicken gate open," said Joseph.

"Close it on your way out?" I asked.

"No time," John said.

"Some of us work for a living," Thomas chimed in.

I dropped the empty ash bucket at my feet and stomped back to the coop. I was sweating from both the heat and anger. But I said nothing, because I owned and commanded my inner self.

Inside, I wiped Richard's runny nose and released him from his high chair while Arlington screamed for my attention from his cradle.

"Clio, can you grab him, please?"

"I'm late for school," he said, heading out the door.

I wanted to shout that I was late, too, but I stayed calmly inside my fortress. That is, until I called for my little sister.

"Ethel!"

The fact that I was following in my mother's footsteps by yelling for Ethel didn't improve my morning.

"Ethel!"

"What, Maggie?"

She'd been standing right behind me.

"Change Arly, will you? I can smell him from here."

She didn't move, and I saw her wondering if she could get out of it. She couldn't, so she did as I asked while I cleared the breakfast dishes.

Mother walked into the room, round with baby and white with exhaustion. "Leave those for me, Margaret Louise. Go get dressed for school or you'll be late."

I put down the soap.

"Arly's clean," Ethel said, plopping him onto the kitchen floor and handing him a candle snuffer, which he immediately began to bang on the floorboards.

"Arlington . . . ," my mother said, not having the energy to finish her sentence. Or even to keep standing. She sat heavily onto the chair at the table.

Arlington kept up his banging.

"Go on to school, Ethel." I removed the snuffer from the baby's chubby hand and he began to cry. "I'll catch up."

I yanked the baby from the floor a little more roughly than I meant to and he stopped crying in surprise. Feeling badly, I gave him a big sucking, wet kiss on his fat neck, just the way I used to do for Henry, and he giggled.

I carried him to the sink and propped him up on the sideboard. "Now sit still," I warned him, "while I do the dishes." And so he'd listen, I began to sing.

"Oh, promise me that someday you and I
Will take our love together to some sky . . ."

He played with a long strand of hair that had come loose from my braid. His chubby fingers felt so good tugging on my head that I kept singing, and washing.

". . . Where we may be alone and faith renew,
And find the hollows where those flowers grew."

When I finished, I placed Arlington on the floor next to Richard and headed upstairs to change for school.

"Margaret Louise?" my mother called, still sitting at the table.

I turned around.

"Thank you."

It was those two beautiful words that had me pull them out and put them on. My reward. My beautiful gloves.

I was so distracted by my hands and arms that I wasn't even winded climbing the hill to St. Mary's. Instead I was mesmerized by the flashes of white as my arms swung, one after another into view. I felt light, new . . . grown. And the best thing was, the gloves had whisked me so quickly up the hill that I doubted I'd be more than a minute late.

A minute late.

The thought had me forget about my gloves for the first time since Mary and Nan secretly gave them to me two Sundays past. Unlike Miss Hayes at Corning Public Union School, being tardy for Sister Greeley was a heinous crime. And between the joy of my mother's gratitude and my marvelous gloves, I had completely forgotten about her. Although now her hard face was all I saw, and I took the last two blocks straight up State Street at a gallop . . . a fast gallop.

The early May sun, not nearly so hot a few minutes ago, slowed me down. And I was sweating in my glorious gloves by the time I reached the front doors of St. Mary's. But I didn't stop. I flew inside and down the hall and swung open the classroom door all in one long motion. A motion too late.

Sister Greeley looked up from her place in front of the class. Her mouth twisted into a cruel smile. My heart dropped so low it made me need to use the necessary. I thought about turning around and leaving, but her eyes held me to the spot.

She waited until everyone had turned to look at me before she spoke.

"Well, well, well, Miss Higgins, so your ladyship has arrived at last!"

Laughter.

Then . . . she noticed my gloves.

"Ah, and I see you've worn your best gloves. I wonder that you even deign to come to school at all."

More laughter. Harder laughter.

The sweet sweat from my run now mingled with the sour sweat of shame as she glared at me in triumph.

After another moment where I couldn't seem to move, I found myself in the cloakroom removing my hat . . . and my gloves. I heard the lesson get underway behind me and silently hoped that Sister Greeley would not look my way again today. My skin, which I'd thought as tough as shoe leather, felt as thin as a whisper. I took a deep breath of musty closet air and reminded myself I lived inside of a fortress, an iron fortress.

But as soon as I walked out of the cloakroom, she began again.

"And here she is, Queen Margaret of Corning." She drew out the word Corning to sound hokey.

The room wobbled and I fell into my seat, squishing down into it, hoping that I blended in with my classmates and the lesson would go on. It didn't.

"Is her ladyship ready now?" she asked.

I wasn't sure she wanted me to answer. If I did, maybe it would be worse because she'd believe I was thinking myself high and mighty.

I said nothing. Instead, I tucked my chin to my chest and stared down at my desk, too addled to take out a book or pen or paper.

"We wouldn't want to rush a member of the important House of Higgins."

Now the laughter seemed to push at me from all sides. I tried to imagine myself somewhere else. The brook. Or in the old barn. Surrounded by every last one of my brothers and sisters.

"Pipe down now, *citizens*," she said, being sure to emphasize my father's favorite word. And her cruel humor was not lost on its audience.

Now I attempted to smile, too, as if I was in on the joke. As if this really was quite funny. But something happened to my mouth. It was stiff and I couldn't control it. I couldn't control my head either, or my eyes or feet or anything, and I just about slipped to the floor while all around me there was hooting and hollering.

Sister Greeley clapped her hands to stop the merriment. "Let's get back to work, everyone."

And then to me she said, "Out of respect for your poor mother, I won't report the lateness . . . this time."

At the mention of my mother—my *poor* mother—I began to crack. I tightened my hold, struggling to stop myself from splitting open. But it was impossible. After all my strengthening tasks, I couldn't hold that other me back.

I stood, knocking my chair into the desk behind me. Sister Greeley, startled, said nothing. Her silence fed me, and I strode to the cloakroom where I stuffed my hat on my head and pulled on first one beautiful glove and then the other. I was nearly bursting out of my head with anger. Every height I'd crossed over, every insult I'd endured with a serene smile, they were all for naught.

Outside the cloakroom, Sister Greeley had recovered, and I heard her yelling. "Miss Higgins. Miss Higgins!"

Now even her voice spurred me on. She was losing control. It was wonderful. But I'd lost it first. And I was not about to regain it. I stepped from the cloakroom and met her eye.

I let her speak first.

"Don't think you can just waltz out of here and then waltz back in," she shrieked, blistering with anger.

"Oh, I won't be back," I answered, allowing her to hear my rage.

She had not expected this, and scrambled for something to say. I took advantage of the moment and waved her a beautiful white-gloved good-bye.

It felt so very good before it felt so very bad. And although I despised that other Margaret—the Margaret who marched out of school—I admired her too, just a little.

Nowhere

The rest of spring and summer passed and I insisted on remaining a dropout. My mother accepted it. She had to. For one, I was not going back to St. Mary's. And for another, she didn't have the energy for a fight. She didn't have the energy for anything. When she went into early labor in late August, she barely groaned through the delivery. She knew—as did we all—this was another who wouldn't live, and she laid motionless in the bed not helping it along.

Twenty-three hours later, Mary and I delivered her a red baby boy small enough to fit in the palm of my hand. Mary washed and wrapped him gently in a clean rag and I tucked a violet between its folds before we buried him in the backyard without a marker. It was yet another birth my father missed.

He worked at the glass factory now, thanks to the successful groveling of Joseph to Emma's father. It was his last option after both local stonemasons barred him from their shops.

Mary and Nan stayed the night.

Mary cooked dinner. Veal pot pie. We sat at the table greedily eating Mary's good cooking. Arlington was shoving the carrots and corn into his mouth, but digging out the lima beans and squishing them in his fists. I didn't like the lima beans either.

It felt like Christmas . . . although a quiet one. My mother was asleep and none of us wanted to wake her. Mostly because she might see how happy we were—all together, and not thinking about what was buried in the yard.

My father sat in his chair and drank his dinner. Gone were the days where he held court at the marble-topped table—feeling our skulls for a glimpse into our futures and filling our heads with thoughts of freedom. The boys and he didn't get along much anymore. I knew it was a choice I was making, to be happy with my brothers and sisters. To rejoice in them, and in Mary and Nan. I missed my sisters so much. Nan's tinkling laughter made the air easier to breathe, while watching Mary's movements from the cookstove to the dry sink to the cutting board was like watching a ballet.

The windows and doors were open. The smell of warm earth beginning to cool wafted through the house. It was late, and we were still eating. Still talking.

But in a lull, Nan sighed. And I knew exactly what was coming.

"What will we do about Margaret?"

It was my turn to sigh. "Nothing. There is nothing to do about me," I said. "I won't go back. I will not go back there. I will work at the factory."

The entire table shuddered.

"You will get nowhere without an education," Nan cried. *Nowhere.*

The word stopped the conversation. We sat in silence. It was where they were: nowhere. It was where I was now heading. One after another, my brothers and sisters had dropped out of school and into hopeless jobs, all the while endeavoring to be the last of us to do this—the older Higginses sacrificing so the younger Higginses might avoid the smoke of the factory, or the backdoor service entrances of the houses on the hill. And here I was, stubbornly choosing them.

I leaped to my feet and walked out the door and into the night. I got as far as the front stoop, where I lost my energy and flopped onto the wood steps. Walking out—it was an excessive emotional display I seemed to be perfecting these days. After all my struggles to strengthen myself, one moment in the presence of Sister Greeley and I was lost.

If only I hadn't stood quite so tall as I made my way out of the classroom. Hadn't said I was *never* coming back, but maybe something like, I *may never* come back. I'd let the me I despised, the me I couldn't control, ruin everything.

Or maybe it had been ruined from the start. Maybe becoming a doctor had always been a silly dream. Ridiculous, even. Women became wives and mothers. Maids. Teachers. Didn't I always know there were no protuberances, no freedom of thought, no vote . . . not even a lousy pair of pants? I'd be lucky if the factory employed me to package up glass for the rest of my life.

My brothers and sisters filed out into the night, surrounding me.

"I have a plan," Nan whispered.

I folded my arms tightly across my chest. "Absolutely no plan will ever make me walk back through the doors of St. Mary's."

"Maggie?" Nan said.

I didn't look at her. I didn't answer her. I was so sick of this conversation. How could they not understand how I felt? Even now, sitting here enveloped by my siblings, Sister Greeley's thin-lipped grin heated my insides to an ashy white coal.

Thomas thumped me on the head, and I exploded. "Don't act like you're the biggest toad in the pond!"

"How can I be?" he shouted back. "When I'm standing next to you!"

Nan wiggled between us in alarm, but it was Mary's tired face of concern that hushed us. She looked too much like our mother.

I drooped in despair. I was letting them down. I was letting them all down. But it couldn't be helped. How could I explain what Sister Greeley did? How could I make them understand the fury I felt? Not only at her, but at myself. The fear that I couldn't control myself. That I never could.

"She . . . pitied her . . . us . . . Higginses." I shook my head. I couldn't let it out. The pressure was too great. And it wouldn't go over well in this crowd, anyway. A Higgins did not engage in tears and temper. We managed. Like my mother in her bed, managing her constant sickness. Her constant loss.

"Yes," Joseph sighed. "Higginses. Her. Us. And him." He nodded toward our father in his chair in the living room. But by the end of his sentence, he was wearing a smile.

"Spawn of the Devil," John added. "Or at least Thomas is."

We laughed . . . even me.

Inside, Arlington cried for attention, and we all wandered back into the house where we had left the babies. Thomas plucked Arly from his high chair and the baby immediately pulled Thomas's rough knuckle into his mouth and began to suck.

"Are we ready to listen to Nan's plan?" Mary asked. "I've heard it, and it's good."

I didn't want to hear the plan. Even if it was one that Mary believed was good. But I sat, like the rest of them and kept my mouth closed, though my mind wasn't exactly open.

Nan became instantly chirpy. She placed both her hands flat onto the marble-topped table and said one word.

"Claverack."

None of us responded.

Mary took over, like they'd rehearsed this. "Founded by Dutch Protestants, Claverack College and the Hudson River Institute is a distinguished coeducational high school that accepts exceptional girls."

She recited it from memory, obviously from an advertisement of the school.

"I don't understand," I said.

"The boys need to pay for Mother and the children. But Mary and I have figured it out," Nan said. "We can afford the tuition if you are willing to wash dishes for the room and board."

"I've contacted them and sent your records. It's all set," Mary announced.

"You are an exceptional girl," Joe laughed.

"Or at least," said Thomas, "Mary has fooled them into thinking so."

Thomas's light jab undid me, and I fell into a puddle on the table, covering my head with my arms, not wanting any of them to see. They were sending me to school? I couldn't raise myself from the table. Even when Mary began clearing the dishes and I heard Joseph head out to feed the dogs. Maybe it was having all my brothers and sisters home again. Or maybe it was another dead baby. Or my mother being so sick, or my father and his whiskey, or Sister Greeley and the rottenness of this town. But truly it was none of these things. I knew exactly why I couldn't face them. Any of them.

It was because of the word exceptional. And how so very much I'd always wanted it to be true.

March 1, 1899

"Go study," I tell Ethel. "I'll finish cleaning up."

And with these simple words, I truly join Mary and Nan. But what better company? All my older siblings have sacrificed so much. It really is my turn.

"Thanks, Maggie," Ethel says.

She's about to say something more but stops herself, although we both know what it is she was going to say . . . that she's glad I'm home. Instead, she dries her hands on a fresh rag and heads upstairs.

My hands are full of grease from scraping the stove when I hear a crash in the next room followed by Arlington's loud whining. Father is in there, along with Joseph and Clio, so I keep cleaning.

Arly's high-pitched complaining continues, and I grit my teeth while I wait for someone to soothe him. What did they do before I got home?

Arlington's fretting finally stops but my anger stays. How quickly I bounce from respecting my siblings to despising them. The anger is so much easier. It pulses through me, hot and alive. Without it, disappointment creeps in, making me feel like one of those dried out husks the citizens of Corning once pelted me with the day Bob came to town. Maybe this is why they were angry—better to holler and howl than to sit quietly in the shadow of pine trees hearing how wonderful life could be, but never ever seemed to be.

Oh how I'd love to despise them all . . . Joseph, Mary, Thomas. Why should it be me here? But of course, why should it be them? And it is them. And me. Except for John, we are all here.

Feet pound across the floorboards toward the bathroom. At least we have indoor plumbing. My heart pinches thinking of Henry and his plumping. If the world were right and good, he would be in there with them right now. If only I were right and good, I wouldn't be such a selfish thing.

All I've done since dinner is move the battle from the outside of me to the inside, and this waffling back and forth between accepting my duty and despising it is exhausting. I embrace acceptance with a long, slow breath, and head upstairs to make quick work of the boys. I leave them rolling around like puppies in the dark where they'll eventually wear themselves down. My only rule is they do not set a foot out of bed or I caution them they will "suffer the torments of hell," since I've washed their feet and am not repeating the labor.

Downstairs I dry and put away the rest of the dishes, wash down the table, and begin to ready the kitchen for tomorrow. Clio says good night next. And then finally Joseph heads to bed as I'm grinding tomorrow's coffee. "Night, Mary," he jokes.

"It won't be so funny in the morning," I say. "When you wake up to lukewarm coffee and burned biscuits instead of oatmeal with sweet cream and warm bread."

He groans.

My father is asleep in his chair, his whiskey glass empty and his book overturned on his lap. From the look of him there, it seems it's where he now sleeps. Good. Perhaps Mother's body will receive real rest without him, or his babies, needing it.

Michael Higgins. He reads and thinks and drinks and lives his life the way he's decided to live it. And no one calls this selfish. They just call him a man. *Always think like this, Margaret,* he'd told me. *For yourself. Always.* I'm given permission to think my own thoughts, just as long as I think them standing in front of a sink full of dirty dishes. A place where all these thoughts can do is smolder and seethe, hollowing me out from the inside. I wish I could stop thinking like *this.* Because I can't be Michael Higgins. I can't even be Margaret Higgins.

And . . . I'm back to despising.

A Good Girl

The morning was so new the dew hadn't yet dotted the sugar maples. I stared out the train window into the grainy dawn at my two older sisters standing on the platform. Nan was smiling, but it was her scared smile. She was afraid for me. Mary was being Mary, so she wasn't smiling, but I could tell by the way she breathed in through her nose how pleased she was. And she should be. Because just as surely as they stood on that train platform, I was standing on their backs. I would not be heading to Claverack if it weren't for them.

The engine released a burst of steam and the train lurched forward. The three of us leaped to attention. But it was just steam. I wasn't leaving. Yet.

Early that morning the three of us had crept out of the house without waking anyone. I'd said my good-byes last night. Father took the opportunity to expound on the demerits of formal education, quoting Bob: "'It is a thousand times better to have common sense without education than to have education without common sense.'" I took it to mean he would miss me. My mother worked harder than usual over dinner, yet looked less tired, which was truly a parting gift. Thomas announced how peaceful the Higgins household would now be with me missing from it, and little Ethel just looked stunned, as if she didn't know whether she should be excited or distraught. Tonight would be the first night in my memory in which I did not have her cold feet stuck to me, and when the train began to roll I pressed both my feet to the floor as if I could stop it. I wanted to stop it. I belonged here. In Corning. With them.

Mary and Nan raised their hands in the air.

"Stop the train," I whispered.

It didn't stop. And I knew I didn't want it to. Not really. Just like Nan, I was scared to death. But there was nothing I wanted more than this. To be leaving Corning, New York. To be heading toward . . . a future? Could it be possible I might actually become the doctor my father always promised I'd be? The train picked up speed and my sisters were gone.

We chugged through the outskirts of Corning, and then dove into the woods. I sat limp in my seat allowing myself to be hurled east. It was a five-hour trip with two changes in trains, but there wasn't enough time to open my book or eat the boiled eggs Mary packed me. There was only enough time to wonder where I was headed, and to revel in the fact that in this very moment, everything felt possible.

My first sight of Claverack, along with the day and night that followed, were like blurry paintings in my head. Trees glowing with a tint of yellow. The windows of College Hall reflecting the

September sunlight. The night's strange darkness in the dormitory where I thought I'd never sleep, only to wake up an instant later to the rising sun.

I stumbled about campus numb with exhaustion the first few days, overwhelmed by the buzzing of five hundred young voices, the routines of the gigantic kitchen where I worked in the evenings, trying to remember everyone's name, finding the location of my next class, and making a thousand new little choices I wasn't used to making. When Betty, who was in charge of the kitchen staff, found me leaning over a hot sink of dishes staring into the bubbles, I readied myself for a scolding. Instead, she laughed.

"You're a marvel, Margaret Higgins," she said. "Go back to the dormitory and rest."

"I'm sorry, ma'am?"

"You're a good girl," she said, patting me on the back with her warm, wet hand. "You've worked hard these first two weeks. Harder than any of them. We're very happy to have you here. Now get to bed."

Being praised for clearing tables, washing dishes, sweeping and mopping . . . this was new. And very nice. I was a marvel!

In the kitchen and dining hall, I mostly felt like myself, other than the heaps of praise Betty and the women in the kitchen piled on me every day just for setting the silverware straight. I worked the evening shift, laying tables and preparing dinner, along with serving my fellow students and the staff and cleaning up afterward. Just like home, it was a world of familiar tasks where one followed the next, followed the next.

Betty had all of us in the kitchen eat our dinners in the same order each evening during the setup, serving, and cleaning of the meal. My position came third, right after Marion, at about the same time the first diners entered the hall. I looked forward to my twenty tranquil minutes alone in the back of the kitchen. I'd never eaten a meal by myself before. There was a comfortable joy in gazing off into the clamor of the kitchen while shoveling in my mashed potatoes and ham. By the time I rejoined the kitchen team, I was refreshed and ready to jump into the fray of my duties.

But I hadn't come to Claverack to work in the kitchen, I'd come to study in the classroom, where I did not feel comfortable or joyful. Inside the classroom I was quiet and withdrawn. If Thomas could have seen me he would have insisted I must surely be dying of some heinous disease.

It had nothing to do with my teachers, who were all gracious and giving. A shock, I admit. The entire teaching staff was brimming with older, more knowledgeable versions of Miss Hayes. They allowed new students like me time to grow accustomed to this humane treatment by calling on the older students and using them as examples. The seasoned students answered questions, gave their thoughts on the assignment, and even asked questions of the teachers in return. To which the teachers responded with delight. It was all very odd and communal and I liked it.

My reservations had nothing to do with my qualifications as a student. Shockingly, my public education in Corning delivered superbly by Miss Hayes, and begrudgingly by Sister Greeley, more than passed muster here. Miss Hayes especially had promoted my love of mathematics and Mary, my love of theater, and I found I was quite on top of these subjects. My history was on solid ground thanks to my father. And botany, my science class, had been so very interesting that I'd not noticed whether or not anyone else was silently panting inside at all the incredible mysteries of the world. It was my initial class of the day, and had my brain whirring by its end.

Likewise, the dormitory was a bright and civilized place where the girls were thoughtful and kind. If you dropped your washrag, the closest girl would quickly pick it up for you. If you stopped to mend your bellows for a moment on the stairs while carrying your laundry up from the basement, the first to appear would ask if you needed a hand. I bunked with three other girls in their first year—Minerva, Hazel, and Vivian. We were all so very generous to one another that almost no conversation went beyond haltingly spoken statements of apology for wrongs not committed, or quick smiles upon entry or exit from the room so as not to disturb anyone's studying with a more time-consuming facial expression. All four of us desperately attempted not to get in one another's way so much so that after three weeks of sleeping across the room from these girls, I did not know what their individual voices sounded like. Strangely, they even slept to themselves, as none of them snored, an interesting tidbit I wouldn't be sharing with Nan lest she believe she was the only girl who did.

Yet even among all this helpfulness and happiness, it was in the classrooms and dormitory where this strange feeling overtook me and wouldn't let go. It was a heaviness that kept me from raising my hand to expound excitedly on my burgeoning knowledge of the reproductive mechanisms of mosses in botany, and stopped me from mentioning the interesting fact that none of us assigned to room 128 snored. Unless I snored. Which I'm sure I didn't. This new emotion pulled at my shoulders, sealed my lips, and weighed on my heart.

It was loneliness.

I'd heard of it but had yet to experience it. Surrounded as I'd been by my brothers and sisters, lonely was something I'd aspired to. Now I understood why most viewed it negatively. It hurt to see so many people I could reach out and touch, but no one waving me over when she spotted me across the classroom or linking her arm through mine while traversing campus. I had become used to missing Mary and Nan, but here in the first weeks of school, I actually missed Ethel.

I worked hard at my studies all day, and even harder in the dining hall each night. My grades and praise were adding up. It was extremely pleasing. But I did wish I'd make a friend. Her name was Esther Farquharson, and I'd been trying to capture her heart since I first saw her.

Esther was a third year. Waiflike. Light of foot. Charming. Intelligent. And beautiful. She pranced about campus saying very clever things. Everyone adored her. I adored her. She was dramatic, and left her long brown hair free to fly down to her hips. Her clothes were fashionable, and she wore them as though they'd grown on her each morning after first enquiring as to her mood and the events of the day. She moved the way I imagined a dancer must move, knowing every step before she took it.

I wanted so badly to be her friend but I'd forgotten how to make one. Or maybe I never knew. Thoughts of Emma dampened my spirit for friend-making even further and kept me far away from Esther.

Amusingly, it was laundry that brought us together when early on a Monday morning she popped in on me in the basement soaking my dresses. She explained how she sent her wet-washing out without her stockings on Friday—like so many of the girls at Claverack, she did not do her own laundry—and now she needed to clean them herself.

"It's Maggie, right?" she asked.

I wanted to correct her, have her call me Margaret because it sounded more mature. But I just nodded.

"Can you show me how to use one of these?" She picked up the washboard with two fingers, as if she didn't want to actually touch it.

"I certainly can," I told her, swallowing my surprise that anyone could not know how to use a washboard.

She smiled. She truly was beautiful.

I rinsed and wrung my dresses, hanging them on the rack out of the way, and then gave Esther a tutorial in what most people referred to as the weekly affliction . . . laundry. However, in the Higgins household, it was a daily one.

"You are such a good girl, Maggie." She laughed when I demonstrated how to use the wringer. Her laugh—as was her comment on my character—was meant kindly. Though both laid me low.

She was right in her assessment of me. Since I'd arrived at Claverack, I had been a good girl. Quiet. Smiling. Existing for others. Like my father's Lady Liberty, I was revealing only my ideal self. The self I'd worked so hard to become.

It was amazingly easy to be this better me at school. Partly it was fear of a new place, and partly being separated from my family for the first time. Although there was something else to being this good girl. It was this something else that depressed me. Here at Claverack I was not a Higgins. I was not spawn. I was not my father's daughter. Here at Claverack I'd been given a chance to make myself into whoever I'd like. Now Esther Farquharson had gone and identified who this was. And though I'd worked hard to cultivate this exact person, I wasn't sure I liked her all that much.

I hid all this from Esther, and she changed the subject from clean stockings to her declamation for chapel the next morning. She was to declaim from Sophocles's great tragedy, *Electra*, taking on the role of Electra at the moment she angrily confronts her mother, Clytemnestra for murdering Electra's father.

Claverack assembled each morning in the chapel. When I first learned of this daily event, I admit my heart sank in despair. I ended up feeling quite the opposite, for in chapel, any student was able to rise and speak, sing, or recite. It was a place where Esther exceled. And tomorrow, she was to perform for the whole school. But this morning while our laundry dried, she performed it for me.

"*'Thou sayest that thou has slain my father.'*"

She was controlled, but I could see the anger bubbling beneath her skin. It was exciting.

"*'For tell me, if thou wilt,'*" she continued, now allowing the anger to surface, and burn through her eyes, "*'wherefore thou art now doing the most shameless deeds of all, dwelling as wife with that blood-guilty one, who first helped thee to slay my sire, and bearing children to him, while thou hast cast out the earlier-born, the stainless offspring of a stainless marriage.'*"

She removed any hint of Esther, becoming fully Electra with the final lines.

"*'. . . for that matter, denounce me to all, as disloyal, if thou wilt, or petulant, or impudent; for if I am accomplished in such ways, methinks I am no unworthy child of thee.'*"

I jumped from the wash boiler and applauded. She was wonderful. Really wonderful. Although secretly I believed I might have done more with the repetition of the word "stainless," and maybe increased the register of the voice when Electra added to the list of insults her mother might denounce her with. And possibly paused for a slight breath before the word "methinks."

Esther bowed deeper. I applauded louder. And then, forgetting all about being quiet and smiling, I stuck my thumb and pointer into my mouth like Thomas had taught me when I was eight, and whistled.

With one shrill blast—I'd made my first friend at Claverack.

Dearest Corey

Esther and I began to meet early each morning in the basement to practice her declamations. She took on the role of every great lady we could think of in theater and literature—too short a list, we often grumbled.

I sat on the edge of the wash boiler playing with the dolly stick while Esther inhabited the greatest lady in the greatest scene in all of great theater—Act One, Scene Seven of the Bard's *Macbeth*. Before she spoke the monologue's last legendary lines, she inhaled slowly, girding herself, and then . . . unleashed.

"I have given suck, and know
How tender 'tis to love the babe that milks me.
I would, while it was smiling in my face,
Have plucked my nipple from his boneless gums
And dashed the brains out, had I so sworn as you
Have done to this."

After which she held her hard, steady gaze on the audience

for longer than was comfortable for anyone to endure, and then plunged into a bow.

I leaped from the copper bucket and hugged myself in joy at her rendering of the beautifully fearless Lady Macbeth.

When Esther stood, her face was red with pleasure. "I may use this for my audition, if I receive one."

"There is no question you'll receive an audition," I told her. She flushed even more.

Esther had applied to Charles Frohman's Empire Dramatic School. She'd only applied two weeks ago, but it seemed as though we'd been waiting to hear back for our entire lives. Esther had dreams. I loved her for this because it meant dreams existed. I'd often wondered if perhaps Nan and I had made them up.

"Will you sit in front at chapel tomorrow?" she asked.

"You don't need me to, but I will."

I wasn't Esther's only fan, so I would surely have to arrive early to secure a front seat for her performance. There were many young men and women at Claverack with whom I would need to compete. Esther was admired. There was one in particular whom I knew would be in attendance. Corey Albertson.

Corey was a first year, like me. He seated himself in the front row at all Esther's readings. When I noticed this, and made reference to it, he told me he was an avid fan of poetry in particular, and the dramatic arts in general. And I laughed.

"Dear Corey," I'd said. "It's strange that I have six brothers at home, and not an avid fan among them."

I had caught him in a bit of a trap. If he pointed out my brothers were not learned men, he might offend me. If he didn't point it out, he risked looking like he was arriving to win a seat up front to witness Esther's performance because he preferred her to other girls.

"We must allow for differences in people," he'd said.

I was impressed with his response. He was smarter than I'd originally thought.

Over the next three months, Corey arrived early to save me a seat up front in chapel for all of Esther's performances: Helena in *A Midsummer Night's Dream*, Ismene in *Antigone*, and Isabella in *Measure for Measure*. During this time, I kept myself tucked inside my good girl character while embracing my growing friendship with Esther. I acted beside her to intensify her monologues. Fed her forgotten lines during her performances. And stayed up nights with her dreaming of life in New York as a famous actress once she had been admitted to Charles Frohman's. Life at Claverack gave me everything Corning never would: Betty and Esther and Corey and ten acres filled with people who had no reason to despise me. Only the weekends left me low, for Esther and Corey, along with most of the students, headed home to visit their families, leaving the campus, and me, feeling empty. Corey thoughtfully presented me with two butterscotches at chapel each Friday, one to ease the blow of Saturday, and the second, to see me through Sunday.

Nan paid for my books and clothes, Mary for my tuition. And I paid for my room and board through my work in the dining hall. There was no extra money for travel. Not that I'd go home if I could, but when everyone departed, I was left with myself—Margaret Higgins, not the good Lady Liberty. I wondered how long I'd play this part of standing around holding a torch, watching life sail by.

Friday evening before my dining duties, I walked Esther to the train to wave her off. Corey was always at the station, ready to board with her. I teased him about Esther not giving poetry readings all the way down to New York. He hardly cracked a smile. He was intelligent, but the boy had the sense of humor of a rock.

By December, I'd fallen into a comfortable rhythm at Claverack. I knew the routines of the kitchen and dining hall as well as I knew the cracks in our old cabin's dry sink. I was excelling in all my classes because I'd made a point to always surpass expectations for every assignment as per the old advice of Dr. McMichael. Esther and I counted each other as best friends. And though he was obviously an "avid fan" of Esther Farquharson, Corey Albertson had become my dearest Corey, as he seemed to be always nearby whenever I needed him.

On the second Sunday in December, and our last week before we broke for Christmas, I took the cold walk to the train to surprise Esther on her return to school. I was bundled up in my overcoat and scarf. It was a pretty winter afternoon. The dying sun lightly touched the icy branches of the trees turning them an amber yellow. Night was falling. There was something about a winter night that always excited me . . . as if anything could happen. Summer nights were for long barefoot walks discussing life. But winter nights were mysterious. And this one felt as if it might be just such a night.

The train clanged into the station on time. Nothing new about this. When the doors opened, a boisterous crowd of Claverack students burst forth. Corey was among them, and was far from boisterous. The evening was following a predictable pattern. What was unusual, however, was that Esther was nowhere in sight.

I hurried toward Corey. When he caught my eye, he balked, springing the hard memory of the moment I'd heard the news of my sweet little Henry into my heart. I stopped short on the platform. Seeing me frozen in place with what must be a panicked look on my face, Corey raced toward me waving a letter in the air.

"She's all right, Margaret. She's all right."

My body turned solid again and I allowed the horrible moment to pass away as I swiped the letter from his hand with a weak smile, my head still a bit wobbly from the scare.

"Thank you, my dearest Corey. You are a most agreeable postman."

"Margaret."

"What?"

He hesitated.

"You said she was fine," I whispered.

"She is."

"Then . . . ?" I ripped open the letter. I didn't need to read the entirety of it to know what it said. She had been accepted. She would attend Charles Frohman's Empire Dramatic School. She would become a famous actress. What she would not do was return to Claverack. Ever.

"This is the most wonderful news," I said, my hands shaking as I clutched at his coat lapels.

Corey made the entire situation worse by leaning into my lips with his lips . . . and kissing me.

I didn't make things any better when I kissed him back.

And when his warm hands gently grabbed hold of my face like having his lips on me wasn't nearly enough, I couldn't help thinking of Lady Liberty standing cold and alone in that harbor . . . and how much warmer it was pressed tightly against my dearest Corey.

Man Is Not the Only Animal

Between the breaking down of Claverack's kitchen and dining room before Christmas, and the need to set it back up following the holiday, I was only in Corning for a week. Although this was longer than either Mary or Nan was allowed home from their jobs.

It was not enough time . . . with Nan, with Mary, or even with Ethel and Thomas. Joseph had moved up in the factory and was now a cutter. Clio, Richard, and Arlington had grown. Clio looked so much like John now it was stunning. Richard was reading. And little Arly was crawling around the house reminding me so much of Henry. My mother and my sisters and I sat over tea and I told them about all my classes.

I didn't tell them about Corey.

My father stuck to his chair, shouting out quotes in approval when he liked what he heard.

"'Until every soul is freely permitted to investigate every book and creed and dogma for itself, the world cannot be free.'"

And disapproval when he didn't.

"'Man is the only animal whose desires increase as they are fed; the only animal that is never satisfied.'"

"We are women, but we shall not bicker with him," my mother said in a low voice, surprising us.

Men. Women. It was a distinction my father had always professed in the loudest of voices should not make a difference in our life's prospects. Although I couldn't help noticing it was the women in his life who began to cook Christmas dinner, while he and the boys did like men, which was whatever they liked, until they were called to eat.

Jumping back into the routine of the Higgins house confounded me a bit. By the time I found the broom and dustpan to sweep out the bedrooms, Mother had plucked and gutted two ducks, Nan had finished washing and hanging the day's laundry, Ethel had washed up the breakfast things, and Mary had made a tart. I could see how much my mother enjoyed having us all home. She stopped working every few minutes and looked up, watching her four daughters moving about her house.

My body was here at home, enjoying Christmas with my family. But my head wouldn't stop thinking about school. Mostly Corey, and his strange profession of love following our kiss. Actually, this was not true. Mostly I was thinking about the kiss, and the ones that followed. But also about Esther and her new life, and how empty the campus was going to feel without her next week when I returned. I even found myself thinking about my classes, my teachers, and my plans of attending Cornell for medical school after graduation. I was surrounded by the familiar movement of my sisters, the playful shouts of my younger brothers, the smell of a roasting duck, along with the general Higgins hum that was home, yet I didn't fully belong to it anymore. Like Mary and Nan, I was a visitor here. So when the week was done, and I was on the train, I found myself craning my neck for my first sight of the Claverack station.

Corey met my train. I suggested we walk the long way back to school, and therefore I arrived on campus with my lips raw and chapped from kissing in the freezing January air. *I was home.* I left Corey to greet Betty and Marion and all the kitchen ladies, and to bring them Mary's carrot soup as a gift.

I was too busy with my dining duties and new classes to miss Esther much in the initial week. Although she stayed on my mind. We'd already written three letters back and forth to each other, so I felt as though I was also starting classes at Charles Frohman. With Esther's permission, I'd promised to pass along all my letters from her to Mary, who seemed almost more excited than Esther that Esther was attending the Frohman school, the dramatic arts being Mary's dream. Between our correspondence, my letters with my sisters, my new classes, my dining hall job each evening, and Corey's constant attention, I began the new term a bit wound up.

Strangely, every addition to my calendar seemed to produce more additions, most especially to my social calendar. Or perhaps it was what I called the "Corey effect." Having a man on my arm had made people notice me. And I liked it.

The acceptance loosened my grip on hiding my Higgins. I began to joke and laugh and tell stories. I began to become more me. Which me I was becoming didn't concern either one of the "me"s—the feeling me or the controlled me—I believed I bounced back and forth between them in a happy way. When I confessed to Corey how I'd like to perform a poem at chapel, he persuaded me further into doing so.

I performed Sappho's "Hymn to Aphrodite." And I performed it well. Afterward, I spent the entire day asking for everyone to repeat themselves when they spoke to me, because I was still back in the chapel, reliving that moment when Sappho's words first fell from my lips: *"Immortal Aphrodite, on your intricately brocaded throne, child of Zeus, weaver of wiles, this I pray: Dear Lady, don't crush my heart with pains and sorrows."*

Even more delicious was the moment when Sappho begged Aphrodite to become her ally in love's battle: *"Some say an army of horsemen, some of footsoldiers, some of ships is the fairest thing on the black earth, but I say it is what one loves."*

As I gloriously relived this line, while at the same time hurrying across the large yard to the dining hall in the dusk, I bumped into something warm and knocked it to the ground.

"Ouch!"

"Did I do that?" I asked, shaking off my self-grandeur.

"Yes, dear Sappho," the warm thing responded.

I helped it to its feet. It was a girl. I recognized her as someone from my class, and was thrilled she recognized me from this morning's performance.

"I'm so sorry," I said. "Are you hurt?"

"Not at all," she responded, smiling. I liked her instantly.

"I'm on my way to the dining hall for work," I said. "Walk me so that I might give you a lengthy apology for tumbling you into the dirt."

"My pleasure." She bowed. "And no apology necessary, lengthy or otherwise, my beautiful poetess."

"My darling," I said, in my very best high-society voice. "Let's be friends forever."

"Let's," she agreed.

It might have been a joke, and I remembered we did laugh. But it became true. Her name was Amelia B. Stewart, and for the next few weeks, we recounted our "bumping into each other" story to whomever would listen . . . a group that quickly diminished over time because this story only seemed to be fantastic to Amelia and me.

Amelia and me.

We were always together. She was clever and happy and adored laughing. At my expense. At her expense. And often at Corey's expense. Although he didn't seem to think she was very funny. I thought he was wrong, as did Amelia.

Amelia was an atheist. Not in word, but in deed. And since my own dalliance with religion had flashed and disappeared as quickly as a shooting star, we got along very well. Each evening after I finished in the dining hall, I met her to complete my studying. She had usually finished hers as she didn't need to work. I studied while Amelia read from the Bible. Those who passed couldn't help nodding with awe and respect. A duo of pious young women working late into the night.

If they lingered another moment or two, they would have received a different version of this scene all together, as Amelia adored exchanging certain words of the scripture with "other" words. Words not found in any holy book. Which was too bad because the new sentences she created were not only lyrical, but quite funny.

"You're such a talent," I told her, trying not to giggle as if I was Ethel's age.

She placed a hand to her breast. "No, my friend, it is you."

We broke down in fits. Corey never studied with us.

I still enjoyed Corey's kisses, but the walk to the location where they took place felt as though it was becoming longer as he filled it with his plans for the future. For a while, I added to this line of discussion with wise and profound advice. But I'd since dulled on it. It had begun to feel repetitive. And when he covered my mouth with his and gurgled how he couldn't wait to marry me, it felt different somehow. Back in January, *marry me* had felt like something strong and deep. Now in February, it felt more like he was talking about a contract.

One day I heard myself saying, "I would never think of jumping into marriage without the definite preparation and study of its responsibilities." And strangely, I actually meant it.

When I repeated this to Amelia, she laughed. She always laughed.

"You can't keep him as a beau once you're in New York at Frohman, anyway," she said.

"True," I sighed, as if this truth hurt. But really, it didn't. It only felt as though it should.

"Okay, forget Corey for a moment," she said. "Open it!"

Esther, along with Mary, had convinced me to apply to the Frohman school. Since the day I'd heard of it, Mary and I had plotted through letters to have me apply. Amelia knew I wished it. This is why she helped me. I hadn't exactly given up on being a doctor, it's just that everything now seemed possible since coming to Claverack. Although I still hadn't mentioned the application to Corey, even though I was quite sure he would advise me to apply. Corey Albertson's passion for words might be outpacing his passion for kisses these days, but the boy was honorable and kind. I was hoping when I broke his heart he still conceded to being friends. I sure did like him.

I opened the application. We stuck our heads together and began to read.

"Name, address, yes, yes, yes," Amelia mumbled. "Audition piece."

We stopped reading and our eyes met. We'd been considering a few pieces, but hadn't decided on one yet. We turned our faces back to the page and continued reading. Amelia finished first.

"As simple as ale, bread, and cheese," she said. She handed me a pen.

I spent the afternoon carefully printing every word, first on a scrap piece of paper and then neatly onto the application. At one point, I felt a little woozy, and discovered it was because I had been holding my breath. I stopped to rest my eyes, and breathe. I couldn't help thinking of Mary. She would have loved to be here right now while I filled this out. Maybe even filling out one of her own?

She was comfortable with the Abbotts, and they loved her. Who wouldn't love her? She was a wonderful person. That didn't change how stupid life was, and life was surely stupid if all of Mary Higgins's promise was poured into some family on the hill. But then I remembered she was also pouring it into me. I picked up my pen.

Amelia walked with me to post it.

"The man born with a silver spoon in his mouth must have been born in stirring times," she said.

"Huh?"

"That was a joke," she informed me.

"Sorry."

"What is the difference between two mermaids, and spring and summer?" she asked.

I shrugged.

"The former are two sea-daughters. And the latter, two seasons."

I smiled.

"Admit it, that one was funny," she said.

"You're right. Two seasons. It took me a moment to understand it."

We walked beside each other in silence.

"Are you quiet because you'd like to hear more jokes?" she joked.

Now I did laugh.

"I'm just nervous about the application," I told her.

"They will accept you," she said. Not too happily.

Strangely, I felt the same.

The Plan

There were ten of us all squished into Amelia's room: Amelia, Minerva, Hazel, Marianne, Vivian, Vera, Rebecca, Leila, Edna, and me.

"They will find us out," Edna said, shaking her head.

"They won't, Ed," Amelia said. "Maggie's worked it out."

"But the window?" Minerva winced.

"That's my favorite part." Hazel laughed. "I've always wanted to climb out a window."

"Who dreams of climbing out of a window?" asked Minerva.

"Hazel Bateman, obviously," cackled Amelia.

Minerva rolled her eyes.

"I'll do it," offered Marianne.

Marianne was our group's quiet one, and therefore no one was ever quite sure of the contents of her head.

"I didn't say I wasn't going to do it," complained Minerva, glaring at Marianne.

Vivian and Vera exchanged a glance. They were sisters. Twins, although they didn't look a thing alike. Vivian was round and serious. Vera was slighter with bright eyes.

"We'll do it," Vera announced.

"Leila? Becca?" Amelia asked.

Both girls took a moment.

"Augie Royter will be there," Amelia coaxed.

Leila enthusiastically nodded her head. I couldn't hold back a dopey grin.

Rebecca held out a tiny bit longer, but finally moaned, "All right, all right."

"We're going to get in so much trouble," mumbled Edna.

"We are not," I said. "I've devised a solid plan."

The plan wasn't so much solid as exciting. Claverack had become my home. And I felt comfortable in my home. Comfortable with my friends. Comfortable in leading all of them on a grand adventure into the night.

Our destination: the Hudson Opera House at the edge of the village, where the upstairs performance hall doubled as a dance hall. The goal: to dance our hearts out with our special admirers.

Corey was in charge of our special admirers. They'd be executing their own plan, which didn't sound as though it needed to be quite as elaborate as ours since the administration didn't keep a close watch on the dormitory across the campus from us. The women's dormitory had eyes on it all the time . . . except for the storage closet window on the first floor, which dropped into a thicket of holly bushes. Perfect cover.

"Ouch!"

"Shhhhhh! It's just holly."

"It scratches."

"Watch out!"

"Well, get off me, Becca."

"Shhhhhh! We're going to be caught."

"We are if you don't shut up."

"Everybody calm down," I commanded.

"Are we all out?" Amelia asked.

"Coming," Marianne whispered as she dropped lightly onto the ground and then arranged her skirt back over her legs.

I counted heads as we crouched in the holly. "We're all here. Everyone follow me." I took a last look up at the dark windows of the dormitory. Lights out had happened thirty minutes ago. Every single window was dark. It was amazing how well we all listened. I didn't see any movement behind the glass. I turned back to collect their gazes, acknowledging we were about to move. And then off I loped for the line of trees about twenty paces from the dormitory.

I heard the heavy breathing and footsteps of my friends behind me. The way was down a little hill, making the going unsteady in the dark. Amelia bumped me from behind.

"Sorry."

I kept moving until I was safely hidden among the trees. They entered the woods in clumps, each one bumping into the existing group of us in the shadows. Once we were all in, I looked back, scanning the windows again for any movement. I saw none.

We mended our bellows, huddling together in the woods.

"This is one balmy-brained idea," Minerva said, but she was laughing.

"You're only two miles from Augie, Leila," Amelia taunted.

Leila's face sobered. All our tails turned down as we considered Amelia's words. None of us had much experience meeting boys in dance halls. I'd been secretly more excited about enacting my escape plan than I had been about dancing with Corey. In fact, this might actually be the first time I'd thought about him since we'd dressed and waited for lights out. I just loved the idea of having everyone counting on me.

I glanced around at them. They were all standing quietly staring up at the dormitory. Part of me was thinking what I believed they were all thinking: maybe we should turn around. It was at this moment that the flaw in my plan occurred to me. How do we climb back up into the window we all just dropped out of? A wave of panic fluttered in my chest.

"Maggie?" Viv whispered.

I breathed. The only course of action I could see right now was continuing forward. I'd figure out the window later.

I waved my hand to attract their attention. "Follow me," I mouthed, grabbing Amelia's hand. She turned and grabbed Rebecca's, and so on, until we formed a chain weaving our way through the woods. Once we hit the road, we released hands and walked, openly chatting since no one at school could hear us now.

The dance hall was a two-mile walk. There was some grumbling about sore feet and frigid limbs, which astounded me because two miles was a hop to the necessary where I came from. I'd give them the cold, though. February in New York was not the easiest of months for midnight walks.

"Is this the right way?" someone whispered. There was fear in the voice, and it got picked up instantly by someone else. "Maybe we should turn back?"

I tried to walk through it, show them I was completely aware of what I was doing, but I could feel them all slowing down behind me, their uncertainty growing. Before I knew it, we were collecting together in a tiny mob on the road.

"Let's go back," Edna said.

"But Augie?" Leila moaned.

"He's not going to marry a girl who shows up unchaperoned at a dance hall, Leila," Edna snapped.

"Marry?" I yelped. "Who is talking about marriage? We're just going dancing."

"It's never just dancing," Edna said.

"It is. I mean, it can be," I babbled.

"It can't," Viv agreed, shaking her head, her frown glowing in the moonlight.

I looked over at Amelia. She didn't look back. For the first time since I came to Claverack, I felt a pang of Corning in my gut. "But we're here to become educated . . . so we might go on to become doctors and teachers and actors."

"We're here to become educated," Edna countered, "so we might educate our children."

The sound of the wind grew louder as we stood on the frigid, empty road allowing Edna's words to sink through our overcoats and into our hearts. Our spirits melting, our faces dropped toward our boots. This was where Claverack led? Back to Corning and babies at worst, or some better town than Corning and babies at best?

"Let's go back," Viv mumbled into her scarf.

"No," I said. "No."

Their eyes snapped up at me in the dark. I hadn't been speaking to them. But now I knew I would, and Sister Greeley's face flashed before me because here I was again . . . and again, I wasn't going to shut up.

"No," I repeated. "No to learning for the sake of others. No to always doing everything for the sake of others. It's as if we don't exist. *Ever*. Yes, our future children, if we have them, are important. Yes, being kind and giving to others is important. But aren't we important? And don't we deserve some attention from ourselves?"

Folding my arms in front of me in defiance, I stared out at each of them. Although I purposely avoided Amelia's gaze, afraid it might remind me of Emma's. Maybe this was the end. Maybe this was where I lost her, too. My heart throbbed so loudly in my ears, and my breath was so raggedy with fear I could barely speak. My last words came out as a thin, raspy whisper.

"I'm going to be an actress. Or a doctor. Or something. I'm going to be *something*, God rot it. And tonight, I'm going dancing."

Amelia clucked her tongue and wrapped her arms around my stiff shoulders, her love coming so fast, I couldn't unwind myself to meet it.

"You already are *something*, Margaret Higgins, but you're not going dancing without me."

"Me too," Marianne added in her matter-of-fact way.

"I am most definitely dancing." Hazel laughed. "Since I'm a much better dancer than I'll ever be a mother."

"My mother is an excellent dancer," chirped Leila.

"Ours, too," Vera said. "She can five step."

"My mother can polka." Edna grinned amid gasps and exclamations and the moving forward of our little group down the road toward our goal.

Amelia squeezed my hand. I squeezed hers back. Things didn't always end in rotten vegetables and spittle, I reminded myself.

We heard it before we saw it. The tinkling of notes wafted across the dark road and a hum of talk and laughter reached us just before we came around the bend and there she was. The dance hall. I had ferried them safely from dorm to destination.

"Finally!" Hazel declared. She was the first one of us to enter the hall.

There was an awkward few moments where we spotted the group we'd come to meet, and the group we'd come to meet spotted us. The strange venue we found ourselves in had made all of us shy, even Hazel. Our two little groups caved in on themselves, becoming more interested in one another than in the band on the stage or the brightly lit hall or the person we'd each just risked life and limb to be with. But the band barreled down on a lively bit of music, and Vera couldn't stop her feet from two-stepping right over to Wallace Thornton, and within three blinks the rest of us followed, pairing off and two-stepping right along with them.

Corey Albertson wasn't bad, once he got going. Not good . . . but not bad. He knew how to mug while he danced, making sure I knew he was doing his best and having fun. I admit I didn't dance very well, either, but I certainly knew how to mug and have fun.

I was twisting and tapping and sweating and grinning when I bumped into someone behind me. "I apologize," I said into the twirling lights of the dance hall.

"Yes, you do," a voice answered. A voice that stopped my dancing feet.

"Hello, Miss Higgins. Mr. Albertson."

"H-hello, Principal Flack."

"Enjoying yourselves?"

Well, we had been. But we weren't anymore. Especially when I saw the lineup of my friends' stricken faces against the dance hall wall next to my Latin teacher, Miss Albrecht. A line that Corey and I quickly joined.

The march back to school was quiet. There were no complaints of the cold or sore feet. Upon return, I didn't remember feeling either. I did, however, remember both the irony of my thoughts on how things end as well as my failed plan's biggest problem—the window—being solved.

Miss Albrecht unlocked the front door using a key on a chain around her neck, and the line of girls solemnly climbed the stairs to enter.

"One moment," Principal Flack said.

The line flinched as we came to a stop. None of us wanted to meet his gaze, but it seemed rude not to, so we did. He stood at the bottom of the stairs frowning up at us. The boys stood behind him, not daring to catch any of our eyes. Not that we caught theirs.

"The nine of you should be prepared to discuss consequences tomorrow."

None of us moved but me. I looked sideways, in both directions. Nine of us?

"Good night," he said.

We filed inside. Up the stairs. Down the corridor. Everyone watching their feet but me. Who was missing?

A shadow caught my eye. I spotted Marianne slinking down the hallway, like a cat, behind us. How had she gotten in?

She saw me, and tossed me a quick smile before she disappeared through her dormitory door. I suppressed a laugh, which would have been highly inappropriate. Marianne Murphy. I would have to keep my eye on her.

Once in bed I let out a giant sigh.

"Shhh."

I was sure it was Minerva. She said we'd get caught and we did. I hated that she ended up being right.

I flopped onto my stomach and went back through the night in my head. Where did we go wrong? Where did I go wrong? What would Nan say if I was suspended? Or worse, perhaps they would expel me. Us. Amelia.

I lay in bed writing a speech to Principal Flack in my head. It was a beautiful thing, and I fell asleep while I imagined myself reciting it at chapel.

The next morning, I was called to Principal Flack's office before breakfast. All my fine language, my rich and sonorous phrases from the night before, flew out of my head. In an instant, I saw how lost I was speaking without proper preparation.

"Come in," he said.

The principal was a small, thin man with a large head and high brows that made him seem often surprised. Although I couldn't see this startled look because he was standing at his desk with his back to me, watching out his office window.

I walked in and stood next to the chair.

"Sit," he said, as if he could see me.

I sat down and my heart picked up speed. His quiet had me panicking. I'd never really believed I would be suspended, but now I was sure I was going to be expelled. We were all going to be expelled. And it would be my fault. I swallowed and swore softly under my breath at my stupidity. Stupid. That was what I was. Not only would I not become a doctor, but I was on my way to becoming an uneducated mother. I grabbed at the chair's side to keep myself from popping out of it in despair.

"Principal Flack," I said breathlessly, not knowing what I was planning to say next but knowing my only line of defense was to be contrite. Very, very contrite. "Principal Flack, I'm . . ." Contrite was something I didn't do well, and I fell apart. "In this moment, sir, I'm seeing some of my very real deficiencies." Honesty I was a little better at.

He turned his high brows my way. I snapped my saucebox shut and stared at him. Waiting for it to come . . . those horrible words that would send me home.

"Miss Higgins," he began.

"Yes, sir," I said, interrupting him. Wanting him to stop talking. To not say it.

"Miss Higgins," he began again. "Don't you feel rather ashamed of yourself for getting those girls into trouble last night? For having them break the rules? They may all have to be sent home."

He was exactly right. It was my idea. My plan. And I loved being in charge. Leading them all through that window. Shockingly, I was contrite, too.

"I've watched you, Miss Higgins. At chapel. In the classroom. Around campus. I've watched you since you came here to Claverack and I don't need to be told you were the ringleader. I've noticed your influence over others. I want to call your attention to this, because I know you're going to use it in the future."

I almost protested that I wouldn't ever do anything again . . . no future planning or plotting, no future anything. *Just let me stay.* But all I did was scoot forward in my chair. Closer to the terrible words about to fall from his lips.

"You must make your choice—whether to get yourself and others into difficulty, or to guide yourself and others into constructive activities that will do you, and them, credit."

"My choice. Yes. I know. I knew. I do," I blurted, thinking of those two "me"s. Thinking of the bridge and the gloves and how I'd tried . . . and failed. My fingers reached for those old lumps on my head, warmly quiet behind my ears.

"You're excused, Miss Higgins. Return to the dining hall. Eat breakfast. Go to class."

He turned back to the window.

I didn't move.

"Sir?"

"Yes, Miss Higgins?" His voice was muffled against the glass.

"The others?"

"Hopefully they're already eating their breakfasts."

I stood to go. My legs, once wobbly with fear, were now wobbly with relief.

"Thank you, sir," I said, never meaning anything as much as I meant these three words. And then I stumbled out of his office.

So . . . he'd left me to self-reflect. Another thing I was pretty sure I wasn't any good at.

"Hope is the only bee that makes honey
without flowers."

The response arrived in a long white envelope. It was thick.
And heavy. Exactly the way I felt as I held it.

Mary. How I wished she was here. Amelia was.

She took it gently from my hands and opened it.

"You're almost in," she announced as she read.

"Almost?"

I snatched at the letter. She whipped it out of my reach.

"Don't be in such a flurry," she scolded, continuing to read.

"They loved your essay. And your experience. It sounds
as if they're excited about your choice of Joan of Arc making her appearance to the Dauphin of France as an audition
piece."

I sucked in an excited breath at the thought of my performance, because I was so good at this piece.

She dropped the letter to her side and looked at me. "You
need to fill out these forms and send a set of photos. Once

they've gone over all your information, and they approve it, they'll send you an audition date."

"This is happening."

I sat down on her bed. Amelia took a seat at her desk.

"I need to write to Mary."

"Let's fill out the forms first. Get things moving."

I looked up at Amelia. "Thanks for helping me with this."

"Thanks for keeping me from being expelled."

"Remember, I'm the one who came up with the stupid idea that almost expelled us."

"Remember, I'm a fully formed person who made the stupid decision to follow you."

We laughed.

"Yes, the forms," I sighed. "And then I'll let Mary know."

My sister would be overjoyed. She brought up the application in each letter. As for the audition, I wasn't worried about it. I'd had so much practice in chapel. I really could be at Frohman before long.

Principal Flack crossed my mind. Strange to think of him at a time like this. He and his surprised eyebrows on his big head. I would have thought it would be Corey who crossed my mind. Of course, now he did.

My dearest Corey. Who hadn't even noticed that the walks to our quiet place to spoon had not included any of that activity in more than two weeks. Who hadn't noticed that all his talking about his banking career had not included me saying much more than "Hmm," in more than three. I took the walks because he was a kind boy and I missed the woods, especially in winter. I'd never admit this to Nan or Thomas, who'd sure chaw over it if they knew. Margaret Higgins, missing a long cold walk through the woods after complaining her entire life about them.

"What are you doing?" I asked. Amelia had a hold of my leg.

"I'm measuring."

"My calf?"

"Yes," she said. "For the form."

I pulled it away from her. "What? You have to measure my calf?"

"And your thigh. Your ankle. Your neck. And your—"

"What?" I ripped the form from her desk and started reading. "My bust size? They need to know the measurement of my breasts?" I felt the blood fill my face even though it was only Amelia and me in the room. "I have to send the size of my breasts to New York? On a form?"

"It looks as though you do."

"Why would they need to know that, or the length of my neck or my ankle? What does it have to do with my depiction of Joan's determination to save France?"

Amelia didn't say anything. Because the question was rhetorical; we both knew the answer. I let the form fall into my lap and we sat in silence.

"Does nothing women do not depend on our bodies?" I whispered.

Again. Rhetorical.

I looked down at the list of measurements that would determine if they'd even consider an audition—the size of my breasts, the length of my neck . . . even how long my fingers were, including my thumbs! And then I plucked the form from my lap, and ripped it in two.

Amelia didn't say a word.

I ripped it in four.

She smiled.

I shredded it into a hundred pieces and tossed it into the air.

"Maggie, for goodness' sakes. Now I have to clean it up. You're so dramatic."

We stopped at those words . . . at the irony of them, and sighed.

"Principal Flack told me I should put my talent into activities that will do me, and others, credit. I think I will disappoint him."

"Because you don't send a boodle of men your breast size?"

"Amelia!"

She shrugged.

"I guess I just love the stage."

"You love being filled with passion. Whether it's as Joan of Arc or Margaret Higgins."

She was right. Amelia was often right. Very much like Nan and Mary. Amazing how it hurt a good deal less when you weren't blood related.

"Have I told you how much I love you, lately?"

"This morning over breakfast when I gave you the rest of my almonds."

"Yes, I remember the moment," I told her. "I really felt it."

"I know you did."

"How will I tell Mary?"

"That I can't help you with. But tell her soon. Hope seems to warp over time."

Again, she was right.

I sat down and carefully composed the letter to my sister before I climbed into bed, and posted it before chapel the next morning. As I was writing it, I realized once again how Frohman was truly Mary's dream, and not mine. I also understood why she'd ask me to perform it for her, as I was her best hope for achieving it. This made me unendingly sad, yet at the same time more determined to make something of my own dreams, even if I wasn't completely sure what those dreams were. For the first time, I felt it was enough to know I had them. Somewhere along the way I'd figure them out.

With the letter for Mary on its way to Corning and the application to Charles Frohman lying at the bottom of Amelia's wastebasket, I actually felt a tremendous sense of relief as I took my seat in chapel the next morning. I still had a letter to write to Esther, whose hope in my following her to Frohman's seemed almost as great as Mary's. I tried out different phrases in my head that I might use to gently give her the bad news as the next speaker stood up at the pulpit.

"Should free-thinking men and the Catholic Church always be at odds?" a young man boomed. I immediately sat up and listened. I'd seen him on campus but didn't know his name.

"If there is a universal truth—and I believe there is—cannot the Church be seeking this truth as well as the individual? We Catholics call this truth, doctrine. And though it may not contain the entire truth . . ."

He paused for dramatic effect. Its actual effect was to give me time to question if partial truth was still truth.

". . . the Church has worked diligently for centuries to identify this truth as specifically and completely as possible."

I wondered at the Church working so diligently to discover a truth that didn't support my hardworking brothers in a union. Or a truth that believed women shouldn't have the right to vote.

"The Church lives only to declare and breathe this truth."

Yes. *This* truth. Not *the* truth. Now I was getting huffed.

"Truth is not true sometimes. It is not true for me but not for you. If it is true, then it is true always and everywhere for everyone, whether or not she understands it."

Had he just referred to women?

And here he gave one last pause. *Yes, yes, yes . . . we realize your next words will be your last. We are not fools. As you seem to be.*

"The Catholic Church, and its truth, is a rock on which to build a worldview."

There was applause.

Amelia politely joined in.

"I'm not clapping for that," I said.

"Maggie," gasped Minnie.

"I shall join her protest," Marianne said, placing her hands in her lap.

Amelia dropped her hands in her lap.

Minerva rolled her eyes, but also dropped her hands. And I knew instantly, I'd be up there on Monday morning arguing against this fellow.

The news spread across campus that I was to present my essay, "Women's Rights," in chapel next week, and the boys, following much of the male attitude, jeered at me wherever I walked.

I was undeterred.

I'd been beaten with overripe vegetables and spurned as spawn. If there was one thing I knew, besides how to do a load of washing, it was how to ignore a sneer. I added to these valuable skills the lesson I had learned in Principal Flack's office: Be prepared.

I found different places to sequester myself to practice my speech—in the library early in the morning, in the basement laundry room, and on my walks with Corey. Corey kept careful watch while I stood on a rock and declaimed for women.

We'd stopped kissing altogether. And I'd spotted Corey on campus in the company of Kathryn Benson. We hadn't spoken about it, but I was happy with the way things were turning out. Kathryn would take over in the career-talk and kissing areas, and Corey and I would be left as good friends. I'd filed this lesson away for a later date: Allow men to believe they've moved on from you, and you are left with a smooth path for retreat without having to deal with their emotions. I adored Claverack. I was learning so much here.

The night before my big speech I couldn't seem to settle. Amelia brought me tea and told me jokes. Thank goodness Marianne was there to laugh at them, since none of them seemed able to penetrate the fog in my head.

"I'm going for a walk."

"It's snowing," Amelia noted.

"I love the snow."

Thomas would have snorted had he heard me say this. But I *did* love the snow. I also loved to complain about it. You can love something and still be annoyed by it. Ethel Higgins was proof of this.

The dormitory door closed behind me. I trudged through the few inches of accumulation and out toward the road. It was cold, and the dry flakes collected in my eyelashes as I walked.

Once I hit the road, I took a left, for no real reason.

The only sound I heard was the crunching of my boots. I stopped walking so I could hear nothing. Closing my eyes, I could have been anywhere. I could have been standing out in front of the old barn by the tracks. But no. I couldn't. Because it wouldn't be so silent. Somebody would be wailing. Like Clio. He was always the loudest of us . . . so far.

I opened my eyes and headed to the cemetery. I'd come to enjoy the company of a cemetery at night since the days of making myself visit Henry's grave. Cemeteries made me feel insignificant enough to be brave.

Struggling through the gate wedged shut by snow, I marched past rows of gravestones until I found a spot next to a group of pine trees. Using the sleeve of my overcoat to brush the snow off one of the monuments, I hopped up and took a seat.

Night. Dark with snow. Among the dead. The perfect place to give my speech. They had nothing to lose by listening to it. No tomatoes to throw. No side to support.

"What do you know about the dead, Margaret Higgins," I whispered.

I shimmied to my knees and then to my feet on top of the gravestone . . . and raised my voice for women's rights.

The next morning, my attempt to grasp Utopia from the skies and plant it on earth did not go over well with the crowd at chapel. The room was thick with frowns and folded arms. And as the passionate words poured forth from my mouth, the audience didn't loosen. Toward the end of my speech, I noticed the young man who had spoken about the truth of the Catholic Church last week sitting to my right. He was smirking. I pointed him out.

"Here sits Mr. Weber, who delighted us last week with his truth. He told his truth, and many applauded. Because it is a truth many believe. And is this the measure of truth? When many agree?

Let me challenge this with another truth many agree with. Things change. Truth changes. So perhaps I am not alone in my truth, but instead, standing at the edge of a new truth. If so . . . every word I've spoken this morning is true. Women should own and control their own property. Women should run their own businesses. Women should have the right to vote." *Women should be allowed to speak their thoughts without being smirked at.* But I didn't say this last one.

I took what I felt was the right amount of time for a pause, and finished strong.

"Women should be equals of men."

Tomatoes might not have flown, but applause was extremely light across the room, albeit exceedingly heavy from a small area of the chapel where even Minerva was breaking a few fingers for my cause.

My heart swelled like an old woman's feet on a hot day. But I needed to get myself, and my swollen heart, to geometry.

"It couldn't have gone better," I crowed.

"Well, the booing as you left wasn't so wonderful," Amelia pointed out.

"And the boy who called you a—"

Amelia put up her hand to quiet Minerva. "You don't need to repeat it, Minnie. We all heard him."

"New Hampshire heard him," Marianne mumbled.

"I've tasted the fruit of knowledge," I informed them.

"We're not reaching her," Amelia said.

"She's too far gone," agreed Marianne.

"And we're late for geometry," Minnie moaned.

"I am floating on a cloud of hope," I chirped. "Hope for new beginnings. Hope for change."

"Hope for arriving to class on time," Amelia sighed.

"Wait. No." I stopped and grabbed the arms of each of my dear friends. "Not hope. Hope, as you pointed out so eloquently, Amelia, warps over time. I am floating on a cloud of conviction."

Amelia grabbed my arm and began to drag me toward class.

"I like it," I said, allowing myself to be dragged. "It has alliteration. I might use it next week on my return to the pulpit."

The three of them groaned, which only served to make my heart sing louder. Because I saw now why Bob spoke through the rotten vegetables. He knew what he was saying was right and true. He believed in it. Standing in front of a crowd and offering up your soul was amazing. Even if they barked and bit at it. One day they wouldn't. Because what I said was right and true. And right and true always rises. Eventually.

"I won't squander away my vision," I confided to my friends as they carted me into class. "I shall care for it, with sweet, sweet vigilance."

My friends took theirs seats. I quickly pulled out my geometry notebook and wrote that last line down. It was good.

Ten minutes into a lecture on perpendiculars and oblique line segments, which I had not been listening to at all, I received a note to see Principal Flack.

Right away.

Nowhere All Over Again

I floated over to Principal Flack's office on top of my cloud, refusing to climb down even if the principal was about to reprimand me for my speech. My thoughts soared even higher than the rest of me. *I will not deign to tarnish my vision with an apology. The truth exists whether it is agreeable to you or not. I think as much as any student here at Claverack, male or female, and therefore I want as much as any student here. I will always think for myself, Principal Flack, always.* And after each new righteous statement, I puffed up further and further, so by the time I knocked on Principal Flack's office door, my noble character was near to bursting out of me, and I rapped so hard, I startled myself.

"Come in," he called.

I took a deep breath, and prepared to defend myself.

"Margaret," Principal Flack said, clearing his throat. Not Miss Higgins. I deflated immediately.

"Please, take a seat."

He was sweating. Nervous. I sat. He didn't.

"Your speech at chapel was wonderful," he said, in the same tone I used to tell Ethel how much I liked her cat drawings. I did like her cat drawings. They were nice. But she drew an awful lot of them, and I wasn't that interested in cats.

He cleared his throat again. Although I didn't care what it was he couldn't seem to say. Because I'd been so sure I had just shaken up the entire world with my speech, and in reality, I hadn't even succeeded in stirring up Principal Flack.

"Your tuition," he said finally.

"My . . . what?"

By the time the second word had left my mouth, I fully understood. He spoke on. "The bursar . . ." Something about "a second term." And, "nothing more anyone could do."

My heart beat too loudly to hear anything he was saying. All I heard was . . . Mary, Mary, Mary. Because . . . the Frohman school. Mary's enthusiasm. Her single mindedness. She was grasping at her dream even as she knew mine was about to end.

I slid back into Principal Flack's chair and stared up into his kind and sweaty face. I was being kicked out of school. I would have to leave here. Leave Amelia, and botany, and the kitchen ladies. But my heart was breaking for Mary. She knew this was coming. And Nan. They both knew this was coming, and they didn't tell me. I couldn't imagine the pain Mary must have been in to not be able to take care of this when taking care of things was what she did best of all.

And now I would need to leave. This dream, this adventure, this beginning . . . was over. Mary and Nan's tremendous effort, my own tremendous effort, had come to nothing.

"Please take your time in collecting your things. Don't feel you need to leave us this afternoon. Say your good-byes in a proper way." He hesitated. As if there was more he'd like to say. But the truth exists whether it is agreeable to you or not.

"You're a good student, Margaret Higgins."

I was so very thankful he did not say that I was a good girl, or that I was promising. *A good student.* This I was. As was Mary. And Nan. I shook his hand before I left his office, clenching my jaw tightly. A Higgins didn't cry. And then I walked slowly back to my room. Very slowly. I knew down deep it was better for me to stay out in the world. To not be alone. Even if it meant I had to pass a hundred sneering students due to my speech, their glares feeling like further proof I didn't belong here.

Where would I go? Not Corning. I would not go back.

I couldn't keep the news from Amelia. And she didn't keep it from anyone else.

"I'd been preparing for a good-bye, but not this one," she cried.

"What about Frohman's?" asked Minnie. "Maybe you can still audition?"

I shook my head. "You need money for Frohman's."

"What about a job?" asked Marianne. "That would keep you from returning home."

"A job?"

"Teaching!" Minnie shouted. "Principal Flack would give you a reference. Even he said you are an excellent student. And my mother knows people in New Jersey."

"Teaching?"

My friends were sprawled across the room, all their good brains whirring in unison to save me. I hid my disappointment at the prospect of teaching, knowing I had always been heading here, to becoming Miss Hayes. A job in New Jersey teaching elementary school was far from the New York stage, and even farther than Cornell Medical School. Although, it was also far from Corning.

"Please write to your mother, Minnie. I'd love that teaching job." But there was no air in my words . . . no passion.

I had the idea I would be teaching students closer to my own age. Instead, the next Monday morning I was set adrift in a sea of six-year-olds. Unlike public school in Corning, where we were all merged into a single class, in New Jersey they were separated by age. And so I now spent my days with eighty-four first graders.

I was extremely thankful to Minerva's mother for the job. I had room and board, and for the first time in my life, I was on my own . . . if being on one's own also included a horde of tiny Hungarian children, for most of my students hailed from this European kingdom.

I saw right off the reel that teaching was a job for someone who knew what she was doing, and that someone was not me. Although I made a valiant effort, setting up my classroom, gathering materials, writing out extensive lesson plans that I pressed upon my young charges day after day. But because English was not their first language, so often they had no idea what I was talking about, and worse, I had no idea what I was talking about either. They were, however, astoundingly respectful for such small beings, and I was amazed by their patience in me as I floundered about trying to teach them something. I had a newfound respect for Miss Hayes.

Every morning I was greeted by a swell of heads bobbing

around my waist, each of them struggling for my attention— aching to show me a craft, share a secret, or relay a discovery. I could barely take any of it in, there were so many of them. I was constrained to a single body, a single mind, a single pair of eyes, and I knew I was wildly disappointing them, though it was the very last thing I wanted to do. Strangely, it was at these moments that my mother often emerged in my thoughts. It was a position I believed she might be familiar with.

The lone spot in the day that both my young students and I looked forward to was our lunch together. It was the only time we spent in one another's company where they were in charge, and consequently, the only successful part of the day. We had all sorts of fun. They taught me the sounds of farm animals in Hungarian and performed folk dances from their home country in which they slapped their boots and danced in tight circles. They were, the lot of them, amazing, delighting us all with their joyful feats. Lunch was a time where words didn't matter and I allowed myself to be one of them.

But it was also the time of day when I was most aware of how wrong I was in this profession. These children needed an education, not a teenage girl's attention, and I didn't know how to give it to them.

On top of this, New Jersey was lonely. I wrote often to Mary and Nan but never letting them know how badly I was doing. I didn't want to further burden them, or worse, cause them guilt for not being able to keep me at school. I never mentioned Claverack in my letters. But there was a fantasy I harbored deep down, that they were somehow pulling together enough money to send me back, and that in the near future, I would return to school.

I also wrote often to Amelia, Esther, and Minnie. But again, I didn't inform them I was wasting the time of a very large group of earnest children. Instead, I wrote them stories of the new dances my students were teaching me, and some of the truly funny things they said. I added in snippets of life in New Jersey, although I needed to use my power of imagination to embellish these into actual snippets since I did not live much of a life here. I was in the classroom six days a week, and mostly slept through the seventh. There were times where I arrived back at my room after work and laid down, only to wake up in the morning still dressed, and therefore, with a pat or two at my hair, ready to return to the classroom.

Even if there had been time for snippet making, the rules for female teachers were a large deterrent. After ten hours in the classroom, I was allowed to spend my evenings reading the Bible, or other "good books" chosen by the women's boarding house—and none of them were good. I was also barred from marriage, or keeping company with men. And truly, didn't the second part of the rule keep the first part from being necessary? There were so many rules. I was not allowed to wear bright colors; my dull dresses were required to reach no higher than two inches above my ankle, and under them I was also required to wear two petticoats "at all times." I always had a snicker when I removed them before bed, thrilled to be breaking a rule. The final rule was both the funniest and the harshest: I was not allowed to loiter in ice-cream stores. This rule would eventually prove to be the most difficult to keep come spring. Thankfully it was the middle of winter, so all I did was laugh when I read it. Although it was much harder to laugh at the weather.

February had seen nothing but freezing rain and snow, adding considerably to my feelings of loneliness and confinement. The climate of southern New Jersey could not compete with Corning in the heights of their snowdrifts or the dips in their thermometer, but it was cold and wet enough that traveling out to discover the world beyond reading primers and arithmetic figuring was nearly impossible.

There was only one saving grace to this place . . . *it was not Corning, New York.*

I stumbled through each day, waiting for what, I wasn't sure. Maybe for myself to admit that this was the end of the line. Here I was and here I'd stay, until—and I shivered at the thought—I found someone to marry me. The only happiness in this idea was I'd get to break another rule.

I wrote to Corey, although I hated myself for it. I knew he still loved me, and I knew I didn't love him back. But he was a decent boy, a kind boy, a smart boy. Wasn't that what I'd been trained to look for? So I wrote to him, knowing perfectly well I was holding up his happiness by doing it.

One would think my desperation would be the result of years of enduring this new life I'd been handed. Instead, I had been here in New Jersey for just three weeks! Three weeks and I was feeling as though someone had stuffed me in a box I needed to claw my way out of. Thankfully I was sleeping well at night due to the fact that I spent my days with eighty-four six-year-olds, and therefore I didn't have too much time to lament my situation before I was returned to it.

Returning to my situation was by far the most difficult part of my day. The sixteen-block walk along flat, well-tended sidewalks felt much longer than the five miles uphill in Corning ever did. It was on this walk that I found it hardest of all to ignore that my dreams were going nowhere. I was going nowhere. And this seemed to be a recurring theme in my life.

I can withstand anything, I told myself on the Friday of my third week walking home from work, against a cold wind struggling mightily to rip the hat straight from my head. *Anything . . . but continuing on in this way.*

But when I returned to my room to find my father's letter calling me home, I realized just how wrong I was.

March 1, 1899

It's late and I'm tired, but I put on the kettle for tea. The boys must have tuckered themselves out because there's no bumping about overhead. Joe and Clio have long since gone to bed. My father is sleeping soundly in his chair. Even Thomas has stumbled home, grunted his good night, and is most likely irritatingly snoring away in his bed with his boots still on.

I fix a cup of tea for my mother hoping she will finally be awake. When she is, it takes me by complete surprise, and all I manage to say by way of greeting is, "Tea?"

I can tell she's just as startled to see me, yet she breaks out in a glad smile, her expression instantly bringing me back to that long-ago day when Ethel laid curled beside her and Mary was the one holding the tea. How I had ached for a moment just like this.

She reaches out for the mug, but before she can take it, pulls her hand back to her chest as her body is wracked by coughing. I clutch the tea tightly, waiting—as I've done countless times—for the horrific fit to end. She hacks and hacks and hacks as if her lungs are filled with broken glass, each inhalation shredding her insides. When she finally drops her hand into her lap, I see her rag is covered in bright foamy blood.

This is the third time my mother has attempted to die. And for the first time, I realize she might succeed.

Locked Out

As March wears on, I become my mother's replacement. I manage the finances, prepare and cook and clean up after the meals, pay the debts, wash the laundry—hill and our own—as well as the hundred other things my mother did, the most tiresome of which is the mending, done late in the evening through strained eyes.

Mend. Patch. Sew. There is a limit to the endurance of trousers.

Ethel is my constant companion, when she isn't in school. We sweat over the boiling laundry, and freeze while pinning it up, taking it down, pinning it up, taking it down. We stand elbow to elbow at the sink every morning and every evening, as well as a few times in between. We scrub hands and feet and pots and floors. Nan and Mary stop by when they can and do what they can.

Father and I don't speak much, but between us, we attempt

to make my mother comfortable in small ways. Father carries her from room to room to give her new prospects while I turn and plump her mattress. We keep the doors and windows tightly shut to prevent any breath of the raw spring air from reaching her ragged lungs. And I spend my nights reading medical books on consumption borrowed from the Free Library.

The books tell me nothing I don't already know. Either bleed and purge, or rest and feed. Since she is as white as a summer cloud and weighs about as much, there's nothing to bleed or purge. Rest she takes care of on her own—all she does is sleep, and cough. Although I do manage to pour a cup of tea and a tin of broth down her every day, her bedpan is the lightest of my sick duties.

Ethel, Clio, and Richard go to school. Joseph, Thomas, and Father go to the factory. Arlington and I stay home with her.

Sometimes I allow him to play at the end of her bed to create an illusion of daytime activity. The constant chatter he keeps up with his toys is awfully sweet. I can see she enjoys listening to him. If I'm going to sit and read, or write a letter to Amelia or Esther, I do it in her room so she feels a part of the living. Because she is living. If barely. Although most days it is obvious this attack is worse than the others, I can't help but hold out hope she will recover. Amelia does too, and keeps me up to date with everything happening inside our Claverack classrooms. We have decided this will help me when I return, a fantasy both of us have decided to support.

I also receive kind letters from Minerva and Edna. I'm happy not to be forgotten. I read all these letters to my mother when she looks well enough to hear them, leaving out the parts where my friends beg to know if I'm ever coming back. It's been almost two months since I left Claverack, and when I close my eyes, I have trouble imagining myself there. In contrast, I never conjure up images of my time in New Jersey, except maybe when my little brothers refuse to listen to me.

"To bed," I holler.

Everyone is asleep but me, Father, and my two ill-behaved brothers. And I plan to be in bed as soon as I finish emptying the ashpan—my most dreaded duty and the reason I always put it off until the last. I'm easing each of the tiny piles of ash out of the pan and into the bucket as if they were fragile eggs so as not to drop one fine speck of it on my clean kitchen floor when I hear their little feet on the stairs again.

"I'll not tell you a fifth time," I warn.

"We're not tired," Richard boldly shouts.

Although the two of them must think better of it because I hear receding footsteps followed by giggles.

Father is reading, and I assume from his lack of involvement, hears nothing. He has replaced his old favorite, Mr. Henry George, with a Mr. Eugene Debs, a union leader who's been very successful in riling up the railway men. Everyone is against Debs . . . the railway owners, the government, the church. Therefore, my father knows he's to be championed. Out of old habit, he sometimes can't stop himself from reading the man's thoughts out loud to no one but Toss, who lies at his feet and is the only one of us left listening.

There is a bang, as if the boys have hit the backboard of the bed against the wall. My father must be choosing to ignore it, because it would be impossible not to hear his two youngest clomping about upstairs like unshod horses. I choose to ignore it as well.

But then there is a tremendous crash, and I fumble my full ladle of ash, sending it up into the air where it spins before clattering to the floor, dusting everything within five feet, including me.

Growling like a dog, I stomp toward the stairs trailing ash.

"Get to bed!"

"No!"

"Richard. Arly. To bed!"

"No!"

"'Intelligent discontent is the mainspring of civilization,'" my father quotes from his reading. He is laughing. *Laughing.* And this is not funny at all.

Exasperated, I fly back into the kitchen, take one look at the ash all over everything, and grab my overcoat.

"I'm going out."

"No," he says, without looking up from his page. "It's late."

"No?" I ask. "No, as in you won't allow it? My free-thinking father says no to his daughter opening the door and walking outside? Well, in the spirit of furthering civilization, I'm leaving."

He looks up from his book. "No, as in no," he says. "Don't I always say what I mean?"

"I see how it is," I snarl. "How it's always been. You are a man of words, words, words. You may say what you mean, but none of your words mean anything. Because you don't mean anything." Without a moment's hesitation, I swing the door open and walk out, leaving it gaping—knowing I've cut him deeply, hoping like hell I've cut him deeply.

I'm through the front gate when I hear him slam the door and lock it. The snap of the bolt echoes somewhere deep inside me. I don't stop, or turn around, but stomp off down the street toward Market because this is the direction my feet are used to and my head is not thinking . . . it's steaming.

He has betrayed me. All his words, his freedoms . . . I thought he was giving them to me. I thought they were mine. But he wasn't giving me anything. In fact, he was taking it away, like he took Henry and Emma and this town, and even her.

My anger requires six long blocks to cool from white hot to red. And another three before I can stop gnashing my teeth.

My sisters, my brothers, they've always seen him for who he is. But I believed him. Even after Henry, I believed him.

I still believe him.

This last thought blows out the rest of my anger, leaving me empty and cold. I stop and look around. I've been so wrapped up in my own head that for a moment, nothing looks familiar. I've walked far enough west that I've actually left town, wandering out into a very dark world.

"Where am I?"

The question hangs in the air, making me acutely aware of both my aching feet and my aching heart.

I establish my bearings and start toward home, each tap of my boot against hard earth reminding me of the snap of the bolt in the door. Surely, he unlocked it before he went up to bed. Surely, he wouldn't leave me outside all night . . . in March, no less. The more I consider it, the less I worry. He wouldn't.

But he would. And he did. The door is locked.

I knock lightly. I know he's in his chair. Waiting. He will open it and lecture me.

But he doesn't.

I knock harder, the sound churning up fear from the bottom of my stomach like a whisk stirring up gravy drippings.

Still nothing. Has he gone mad?

I sit down on the steps and hold my head in my hands to stop it from feeling so strange. He has locked me out. Locked me out. For what? For taking a walk? For not listening to him? I've spent my entire life listening to him. I'm the only one who ever did. I listened and I repeated and I learned and I worshipped. I *worshipped* him.

How dare he.

I will the anger back again. But it doesn't come. And I'm left shivering on the steps.

My choices are limited. The only room I could possibly climb into is my mother's, but I will not wake her from her sickbed sneaking through her window. The Abbotts are less than two miles. All uphill. Mary's room is in the servant's wing off the back of the house. She'll be awake reading. And if not, she's a light sleeper.

By the time I reach the Abbotts I'm stiff with cold. The warm night is still a March night. I use a branch I found on the way up the hill to scratch at Mary's pane.

She looks out, and when she sees me in the yard her eyes go wide.

I meet her round the back door, and follow her silently to her room. She closes the door and helps me out of my coat.

She loans me nightclothes and tucks me into her bed. I pretend to fall asleep before she joins me. I don't want to explain. Not tonight. Maybe not ever.

I lie awake for what feels longer than any of the days I spent inside my New Jersey classroom, listening to the strange clicks, creaks, and squeaks of the Abbott house. It's been forever since I slept next to Mary's warm body, but the familiarity of her can't dispel how out of place I feel.

Where do I want to be right now? Claverack? The old cabin? Across the room from Ethel? The trouble is, I don't want to be in any of these places, including the one I'm in.

But I will go home. I have to. For her.

I wake while it's still dark.

"Maggie?" Mary asks sleepily.

"Go back to sleep."

She doesn't listen, just climbs out of her warm bed and we dress together. She hands me a clean towel, and I wash my face with cold water from a basin on her dresser. I don't bother with my braid.

She lets me out the same door I came in. "I'll stop by tonight," she says.

"No," I tell her. "I'm fine."

She doesn't say anything, but I know she'll be by tonight. I know my sister.

The walk down the hill wakes me up. The door is unlocked. I'm boiling the water for coffee before anyone is even out of bed.

He is the first one awake.

He stands in the kitchen behind me while I work. I know he is there. And he knows I know he is there. Yet we say nothing to each other. The door to the connection we shared has been closed for so long, and now, I have bolted it shut.

Rosemary and Rainwater

"More?"

It's the first time she's finished an entire bowl of broth since I've been home. A good sign.

"No, thank you," she says, weakly, but not in a whisper. And not followed by a coughing fit.

I remove the bowl to the kitchen and put on the kettle.

It's raining. The laundry is hung all over the tables and chairs around the house since there's no little one to tug it down, as Mary has taken Arlington out for the day with the Abbotts' youngest. Clio, Richard, and Ethel are at school, and Father and the boys are at the factory.

I bring her tea and sit down beside her.

"I've been invited up to Buffalo for Easter weekend by my friend Minerva from school," I tell her. "I could attend the liturgy at St. Mary's on Friday morning, and then take the noon train up. I'd be back on Sunday evening." I know it will make her happy if

I attend Good Friday service. "Mary said she could come Friday night through Saturday, and Nan from Saturday until I arrive home on Sunday."

She pats my hand. "You should go."

I'm glad she's given me permission. I've been stuck in this house for almost a month. I need a couple of days away from here. Away from my father.

We sit together listening to the rain drum on the roof.

"Nice," she says.

"It is, isn't it?" I smile.

"Do you have the buckets out?" she asks.

"We have running water, Mother."

"You know I like the rainwater."

I get up and collect a few buckets, and set them out the back door. She's asleep when I return.

No matter, I have work to do.

It seems I'm forever either on my knees before a grate or leaning over the sink. I'm sweating like a blower dog by the time I'm finished turning the mattresses and making the beds. I come downstairs, put the kettle on again, and then check on my mother.

When I enter the room, she's sitting up in bed with a bit of life in her green eyes.

"Hi," I smile.

"Are the buckets full?"

"I'd completely forgotten about them. Let me check."

The rain has been falling steadily all day and each of the buckets has a few inches in it. I report the amount to my mother.

"That's enough," she says. "Bring them in."

"Am I to wash your hair?" I ask.

"I'm to wash yours," she says.

I roll my eyes. But I haul in the buckets. There is nothing she asks of me I won't do. I can't stop the pain or the coughing or the course of this accursed disease, but I can fetch rainwater.

I pour all three buckets into the large cooking kettle and start to warm it on the cookstove. Then ready the porcelain basin, soap, and towels.

I hear the bed creak.

"Don't get up, Mother. I'll bring it to you."

"I'm right here," she says, scaring the wits out of me at the door to her bedroom.

I rush to her. She waves me away. "Let me be. Let me be. I'm fine." Although the word fine barely makes it from her lips.

"Please," I beg.

She inhales, but does not cough.

"At least sit."

She listens.

Once the water is hot, I pour the basin full.

She gives me a look. I sigh. "All right, all right." I remove my dress, unbraid my hair, and sit back at the table. She rolls up her sleeves.

The rain beats on the roof as she works the soap into my hair. "I love how soft the rainwater is," she says, so quietly that I'm not exactly sure I didn't hear it right through her fingertips.

My scalp tingles from her gentle scrubbing and my feet throb from being off them. The smell of rosemary surrounds me from a sprig she steeps in the hot rinsing water. The sleeve of her nightgown slips back and forth across my nose, and I can hear her gentle breathing as she works. I'm in the kitchen sitting at the marble-topped table, but I'm also drifting off. To the old bedroom in the cabin. On an imaginary day long ago—a day without croup. Without O'Donnells. I am lying comfortably warm in the bed beside her. Finally.

"I feel your protuberances," she says, her words bringing me back to the table. I know what she's doing. She wants me to forgive him. Like she has, all her life.

"What good are they?" I say, not looking at her . . . or for an answer.

"Margaret Louise," she says. Just my name. As usual. But for the first time in my life, I'm not sure I understand its meaning.

A Beautiful March Morning

Friday comes and my mother insists she's well enough for me to leave. Joseph, Ethel, and I corral the boys, including a complaining Clio, and head to St. Mary's. The boys usually don't attend Mass, but it's Good Friday, and we can't leave them at home with just my father to care for them. Joseph carries my suitcase. Thomas carries his fishing pole, as he is only tagging along until the turnoff for the brook.

At the last moment, I allow Clio, Arly, and Richard to go with Thomas. Why not?

I'm highly praised for my decision before the boys jog off, something I haven't had from any of them . . . ever.

Joseph, Ethel, and I continue on for another few paces, but I can sense Joe's desire to be with his brothers.

"Why don't you go fish, Joe? I can carry this. It's only got my nightclothes."

"You don't mind?"

"Not at all," I tell him.

While Ethel and I watch him trot off, I spot a patch of pretty white trillium. I make a plan to return for the wildflowers on my way home on Sunday evening. Mother will love them.

It's a beautiful March morning—the last day of the month. The sky is clear and blue. The air is light and not fogged over from the furnaces of the factory. It's cool enough to make you feel happy to be out, but not in the least bit uncomfortable. It's the kind of morning that has you looking forward to a hundred more just like it.

Nan, Ethel, and I sit in the back by the beautiful statue of Mary. Our Mary sits with the Abbotts up front, as usual. We will see her at the end of the service.

It's my first time in St. Mary's since I've returned to Corning, and when I catch sight of Father Coghlan, I'm shocked at how much older he looks. Although I find his stamina for the service undeterred by the aging process, and thus have plenty of time to wander about in my head, as well as take in the familiar faces of Corning. I hate them all a little less this morning. Maybe it's the beautiful weather, and summer on its way. And Nan sitting next to me, with Ethel on my other side. And that my brothers are fishing. And my hair smells of rosemary and rainwater.

It is folklore that a consumptive who survives through the month of March will go on to continue living. My mother dies on the thirty-first.

When Minerva meets me at the station, it is not to pick me up for a lovely weekend of planning our futures, but to return me to Corning with the horrible news. She had packed me dinner, bought my ticket, and placed me on the first train home with more hugs than I'd ever thought possible in an hour. Not that I felt any of them.

I had not been at my mother's side, just like the day Richard was born. And just like that day, I would be the last one to her. I'd gotten on the train. Why had I gotten on the train?

On the ride west, I had daydreamed of returning to school and catching up with my classmates. Minerva's letters had even spoken of the group of us heading to New York City after graduation and becoming nurses. It seems Esther's mother has a contact.

On the ride east, I sit stiffly in my seat with a dinner on my lap and a suitcase by my side, feeling as though I exist out of time, and therefore, as if anything is possible . . . like finding out all this is a misunderstanding.

Thomas is waiting for me at the station, and the faraway look in his eyes tells me there's been no mistake. We rattle through the streets of Corning, every clank and shout penetrating me like a dagger. The closer I get to her, the more deeply I feel every rut in the road.

Thomas drops me off in front of 308 East First Street for the second time in a month, and for a second time, I stumble through the gate and up the flags. Clio and Richard sit clumped together on the front steps, a dark heap of boys I barely glance at as I pass. Nan meets me at the front door. Always Nan. She takes my hand and leads me toward my mother's room. My sisters have already laid out her body. Just as they had Henry's. And on the very same bed.

It has happened. She has died. She is dead. Her body lies still on top of a perfectly made bed. Her hair is brushed and braided into a crown. She is wearing a dress I recognize only from seeing it folded up in her bureau. She is wearing her boots. They've been shined. The warm, wet messiness of life has been replaced by the cold, dry neatness of death.

Mary closes the door, closing the five of us in, and I go to my mother . . . grab her cold hand, but then drop it. Touching the dead is always a mistake. I hear Ethel sob behind me. My mind swims in the quiet of the room, and before I can stop myself, I think it. *Did she love me?* I wanted her to love me. More than anything. It's normal to want your mother to love you. Everyone wants this. Everyone needs this. But is it normal to wonder if she had? Did most people just know the answer to this question? Maybe a mother said the words "I love you." Maybe she'd thrown her arms around you, kissed your cheek. Maybe she had long conversations about her life. About yours. Maybe you just knew. And I didn't. I didn't know.

Margaret Louise, she'd said. With sadness. So much sadness.

Where It Ends

We bury her two days later. Inside the churchyard. My father says nothing about this decision, but stands crumpled beside us.

Afterward, wearing borrowed black dresses from the Abbotts, we serve an angel food cake Mary had baked for the parish bazaar to Father Coghlan and his assistant, the O'Donnells, and a host of hush-speaking women from church. So many people. So many dirty dishes.

That evening, Ethel and I stand shoulder to shoulder at the sink late into the night. The next morning, we pack up the dresses and say good-bye to Mary and Nan, as they need to return to their jobs. And just as if it were any other day—and strangely, it is—we prepare the lunches for work and school.

"Don't worry about mine," Ethel says.

"I'm making yours," I tell her. "You should go."

Ethel sits down at the marble-topped table, too tired to move, while I wrap up potato bread and cold ham. I want her to go. I want them all to go. I want to be alone here, at least alone with my own thoughts, as Arly is going nowhere.

Ethel staggers off to school with Clio and Richard, while Joseph and Thomas head out to the factory. Father remains in his chair, where he stays for weeks.

He is inconsolable. Although none of us try. Because there are groceries to buy, meals to prepare, boys to feed, trousers to mend, and laundry to wash. As there always is. And I throw myself into these things. Even going well beyond the usual cleaning by washing the windowpanes, dusting the mantel, greasing the knives, trimming the lamps, and polishing the silver.

I spend my days in the same filthy dress, my braid pinned up and under a scarf, for what feels like months. I don't bother to wash, but simply sleep in my dirt. The more he sits with his face in his hands, the harder I work. I want someone to stop me. Someone to tell me to wash myself. To rest. Of course, no one does. So, I keep cleaning. Feeling empty inside. The lightness of it making it easier to whisk around the house.

He does not return to the factory. He makes camp in his chair. Irritable and demanding. Whatever I do, it can be done better. Ethel, as well. We work harder and harder, giving him more to complain about, more to criticize. We attempt to keep Clio, Richard, and Arlington away from him, sending them off to help Joseph, or on some errand . . . even early to bed.

We settle into our new life, Ethel and I a team—a tired and beaten team—and my father against us, growing stronger every day in his discontent. This is the way we mourn her. Through anger and despair.

Is there any other way?

★ ★ ★

When summer comes and school lets out, Ethel is home, and my team is fortified. We throw the boys out of doors every morning with Clio to watch out for his younger brothers. They often bring back a bucket of pike, or a few freshly killed hares, and I amaze myself at how easily I can now crack the legs of a rabbit and rip its skin from its back. When I describe these successes to Amelia, Esther, and Minnie through my letters, I can almost hear their horrified laughter through the post. Although when I describe my successes to Mary and Nan after Sunday Mass, Mary shrugs. "Anyone can skin a rabbit, Maggie."

Minerva couldn't. Ever.

"Allow her some pride in her work, Mary," Nan says.

"I'll be proud when she skins her first bear." Mary snorts.

"Mary!" Nan gasps.

"She's joking, Nan," I say.

It's been months since Mother died, and I haven't missed a single Sunday . . . it's the only time I'm able to visit with Mary and Nan.

In these small moments with my sisters we talk about cooking, the little dramas up the hill at the Abbott house, speculating on how John is getting along out west, or how annoying Clio can be. We never mention Mother. We never mention Father. And we never mention becoming actors or writers or doctors, or even speak the word "school." Until Mary finally mentions it, but in context of Arlington, not me.

"I've registered Arly at St. Mary's for the fall," she says.

With this single line, I know. My education is over. This is it. This is as far as I go. And I should have known this already. Of course I should have known. I'm so angry at myself for not knowing. For not seeing.

"Where is Ethel?" I snap.

I need to leave. To be alone. Or at least to be with just Ethel, which is almost as if I'm alone, we've been together so long.

"She's always running off somewhere these days, isn't she," laments Nan, without much thought.

Nan's right. Ethel has been running off lately.

"Well, I'm finished waiting for her. Tell her I've left."

Nan recognizes my anger . . . my pain, and grabs my arm. But I can't look at her. I remember her moment, on the way home from school, when she realized that was it. That was where it ended for her. Where it ends for every one of us. My mother, Mary, Nan, Emma . . . and now me. The moment we realize our life has become someone else's laundry.

"Maggie," she says.

"I have to go."

This is my moment. And I want it alone. I squeeze Nan's hand and walk off. She deserves at least this.

Neither of my sisters will chase me down, burst out in emotion, tell me I'll make it, that I'll become the doctor I'd always thought I'd be. There is no reason now, anyway. My only reason to study medicine is dead. We'd both lost our battles.

"Maggie!" Ethel calls.

At the sound of my little sister's voice I stop and turn. I'm a couple of blocks ahead of her. I wait for her to catch up, thankful she's here.

"Where were you?" I ask as we turn and continue walking.

"I'm seeing someone," she says.

"What?" I say. "You're only twelve."

"I'm almost sixteen, Maggie."

"Almost."

"It's Jack Byrne," she reports.

I stop walking and stare at her. "Jack Byrne!"

"Oh, Maggie. You know it doesn't matter whose name I say; you're just horrified because he's a Corning boy."

The truth stings. I quickly bury it under further outrage. "But Jack Byrne? Ethel!"

"He's got a nice . . . smile."

I roll my eyes while I attempt to remember Jack Byrne's "smile" from Mass. "What could you possibly talk about with that boy?"

"We don't do much talking." She laughs.

"Ethel!"

"Maggie, you're behaving just as Nan would. I swear, I thought you'd be happy for me."

"I am acting like Nan. And I am happy for you." I smile.

"Oh my," she says. "Now you're not behaving like Maggie."

We laugh, and she takes my arm and we start for home. Ethel and I, shoulder to shoulder, elbow to elbow. I sigh and lean in to her. If I am to be chained to Corning, I am chained in good company.

"Maggie?"

"Hmmm?"

"I'm going to elope."

I let go of her arm and back away.

"Maggie?"

I shake my head, willing her to be quiet. She's leaving me. She's going to get married. Ethel. Married.

And I'll be alone.

She throws her arms around me. I don't hug her back, but I allow her to hold me. I need her to hold me.

"Why?" I ask, my question muffled by her embrace.

"I have to get out."

I nod against her shoulder.

"When?"

"Soon."

"Does Mary or Nan know?"

"Just you."

"And Jack," I add.

"And Jack," she says.

"Maggie," she whispers. She knows. She knows she's leaving me. Alone. With him.

"I'm all right."

But I'm not. I'm not all right.

Somehow, though, I manage to look like I am all the way home—then on through to the night, and into the next day. One moment at a time. One day at a time. One disappointment at a time. I manage to pretend everything is all right. I manage. To not think about how slowly, slowly, slowly this is all becoming quite normal.

March 1, 1900

The winter has come and gone, just as it seems my life is doing. Best not to think about it. Best to do as my mother did. As the world says to do. My duty. It's incredibly easy to do. It begins on a Monday and follows into Tuesday, and before you know it, you're counting off the week, the month, the year. My only goal each day is to arrive at the place where I might finally sit and read the next novel I have borrowed from the Free Library.

Ethel leaves for Jack. My brothers leave for school or factory. I run the house. And my father migrates from his breakfast at the marble-topped table to his books and papers at his chair. Eugene Debs has grown in fame and deed, and so has grown in my father's estimation of him. Our house fills with Socialist papers. He is also digging into psychology. Between the two of us, the books pile up.

With Arlington in school and my mother in the grave, it is

he and I during the long days. It does not escape my heart how much my younger self would have loved this.

"What have you got there?" he growls.

I shift my position in the chair so he can't read the title of my novel.

"Look here at what I'm reading," he demands.

I know what he's reading. He's reading *The Social Democratic*. He's always reading *The Social Democratic*. I do not look.

"Now here is a man worth reading," he continues, shaking his paper at me. "Not the ninny you're holding."

He drones on. But I don't listen. I've heard this speech before. Yesterday. And the day before that. He believes novels are foolish.

". . . an uncultivated mind . . ."

He is difficult to shut out.

"Read what will benefit you in the battle of your life," he admonishes.

"I *am* reading what will benefit me in the battle of my life. *The Three Musketeers*. And it's doing just what I want it to do— taking my mind away from here." At this, I remove myself to the kitchen, because not even Alexandre Dumas can drown out the annoying brogue of Michael Higgins.

"I see you are agitated, Margaret," he shouts after me. "'Progress is born of agitation,' as the good Mr. Debs has said. 'It is agitation or stagnation.'"

I plop myself at the kitchen table and attempt to read, but the word stagnation has me slamming my book down on the cool marble and walking about the floor. And of course, now I am agitated. Making my father right. Which makes me even more agitated.

I stomp over to the cookstove to put the kettle on, but stop. I don't want tea. I look around the kitchen for what I do want, but I know what I want isn't here. What I want is . . . beyond here.

I sigh, and turn toward the window and look out into the rainy gloom just as I had once looked in through a window on another gloomy day long ago.

"Mother," I whisper, so lightly the word doesn't fog the glass.

I'd do anything to see her reflection behind me. Moving through the kitchen, a baby on her hip, one in her belly, and coughing, even. I'd take her coughing. But the only reflection I see is my own. Silent and still, my long braid neatly plaited and resting over my shoulder, looking very much as if it had been carefully placed there, looking very much like her.

Without thinking, I pick up Mary's butchering knife and saw through my braid. Hair being sliced through by a knife turns out to be one of the loudest sounds I've ever heard. I stare at the rope of it in my hand. What did I do? What did I just do?

I fling the braid and the knife onto the table, clapping both my hands to my head. My head without a braid. A braid I've worn all my life.

I look up at my reflection in the window and gasp . . . a real Nan gasp, which makes me laugh. I shake my head and my hair puffs wildly around my shoulders. Staring at this unfamiliar girl in the window, I realize that she too wants something beyond here. Of course she does. We all do.

Mary longs for the stage. Nan burns to write. Every girl I know—Emma, Esther, Amelia—has wanted something beyond . . . perhaps even my mother. Wanting it, though, is one thing. Being able to choose it is quite another. And maybe this is what every girl *should* know—there is no freedom without choice.

Making the choice to live the life I want to live, the life I need to live, is true agitation. Progress might be born of agitation, as Mr. Debs, said, but I know how much more there is to agitation besides progress. Hard things. Like a beet thrown at close range, and the cold, uncaring eyes of an entire town.

Margaret Louise.

I don't know what lies beyond. Neither did she. But she knew I'd go. Beets be damned. Maybe this was the reason she sounded so sad.

I arrive on time for the earliest train with everything I own: a valise carrying two dresses, three pairs of knickers, a nightgown, and of course, my beautiful silk gloves—all neatly folded and packed. My coat is buttoned to my chin to keep out the raw cold of spring. My boots are laced up tightly. My face is washed. My hair, free. Anyone witnessing my clipped stride as I walk down Market Street would have no other choice but to agree, I look like someone who is on her way to challenge the world.

Historical Note

Margaret Louise Higgins Sanger (1879-1966) left home at twenty and entered into an accredited three-year nursing program at White Plains Hospital in White Plains, New York. Nursing was not respected then as it is today. It was considered equal to being a house servant—a job Margaret knew all too well.

As a visiting nurse on Manhattan's Lower East Side, Margaret witnessed the despair, sickness, and death brought on by unwanted pregnancy, self-induced abortion, child abandonment, and child labor. In essence, she saw aspects of her mother's life playing out over and over again inside the tenements, a life she had desperately tried to leave behind. It was here that Margaret realized her mission—not as a doctor in the service of her mother, but as an activist in the service of all women.

Margaret began her crusade by speaking, writing, and distributing pamphlets and information on female sexuality, sexual education, and contraception—coining a new term: "birth control."

These actions were not only considered obscene at the time, but were also illegal. She was arrested in 1914 and fled the country to avoid prison, living in exile in Europe for a year. She returned in 1915 to fight the charges against her, and to open the first American birth-control clinic, beginning a long battle to make family planning and sexual education part of regular health care. For this, too, she was arrested. And this time, she served thirty days in prison.

But Margaret continued her work. She went on to launch the first legal family planning clinic, promote new contraception (notably the birth control pill), and to fight for a woman's right to control her health and reproductive future—none of which was without controversy. It didn't help that Margaret remained the same person who thought it was a good idea to cross a train trestle high above the Chemung River. Margaret not only attempted to acknowledge a woman's sexuality, but proclaimed women had the right to have sex for pleasure, an absolutely unacceptable concept in early 1900s America—and an idea women still fight for today.

Margaret defied the conventions of society, and for doing so, she often paid with her reputation. Her refusal to live the socially conventional life expected of women brought harsh judgment from the society she rejected. This harsh judgment still follows her legacy today. Most of the vitriol aimed at Margaret personally, stems from her advocacy of eugenics.

Eugenics was a widely held scientific belief in Margaret's lifetime that aimed to improve the genetic quality of the human population. Margaret was a eugenicist, as were Theodore Roosevelt and Helen Keller, among many others. In this time period, eugenics could be found in the high school science textbooks of more than half the states in the country. Today, we realize just how ableist, racist, and sexist this thinking is. It is from eugenics that the horrendous idea of sterilizing certain women—namely women with disabilities and women of color—arose.

Margaret did advocate the sterilization of what was then medically termed the "mentally unfit." She defined these as people who could not properly care for children due to disease or disability, citing alcoholism and severe mental illnesses such as schizophrenia. She was far from alone in this view: The majority of the medical community agreed with her, as did the U.S. Supreme Court, which ruled in favor of sterilization of the "unfit" in Buck v. Bell in 1927, with only one judge dissenting. A ruling both Robert Baldwin of the American Civil Liberties Union and W. E. B. DuBois of the NAACP agreed with. This view was partly due to ignorance at the time about the nature of mental illness, and partly due to the lack of treatment options. There were few medications available for people with mental illness, and often the solution was a lifetime of institutionalization.

Although it is true that Margaret did believe in sterilization of the "mentally unfit," her detractors took this view—a view we realize today is unacceptable—one step further, stating that she also applied this idea of sterilization to races and religions, and thus deemed her a racist. This is false. As Margaret wrote in 1934, "If 'unfit' refers to race or religions, then that is another matter which I frankly deplore."

Margaret was actually a progressive thinker on race for her time. She opened her clinics to both black and white families and would not hire any nurse or doctor who did not agree to treat patients of color. The power structure that wanted—and still wants—her reputation ruined constructed a racist version of Margaret, hoping it would damage her message. To this end, Margaret's words were often taken out of context to purposely distort her views on race, and thereby detract from her mission. One quote used repeatedly to attack her came from a letter written to a donor about the Negro Project (a name that reflected how black Americans were commonly identified at the time).

The project was an effort to bring birth control and healthcare to black Americans in the south who were being neglected by the public healthcare system. It was supported by W. E. B. DuBois of the NAACP, as well as by Mary McLeod Bethune, founder of the National Council of Negro Women. In this letter, Margaret wrote about how she was encouraging more community involvement—by training black ministers in outreach so they might aid in the recruitment of black doctors and nurses for the project—because she feared the project might be misunderstood if it was solely run by white people. She ended these thoughts with the sentence: "We do not want word to go out that we want to exterminate the Negro population and the minister is the man who can straighten out that idea if it ever occurs to any of their more rebellious members." What she meant was this: The last thing we want is for anyone to think our goal is to exterminate black Americans. She was worried that anti-birth-control advocates would undermine the project, painting a sinister picture of it. Ironically, using the first half of this quote, they did just that.

Three more quotes wrongly attributed to Margaret are still used today to spread a false racist persona of her. The first is a quote from W. E. B. DuBois: "The mass of ignorant Negroes still breed carelessly and disastrously, so that the increase among Negroes, even more than the increase among Whites, is from that part of the population least intelligent and fit, and least able to rear their children properly." The last two are: "More children from the fit, less from the unfit—that is the chief issue of birth control," and "Colored people are like human weeds and have to be exterminated." Margaret simply never said either one.

Margaret's personal and political faults were—and continue to be—exaggerated and misrepresented by those who wish to sabotage her message: that "Women should have the right to control their bodies, and therefore, their lives." This doesn't mean her faults should be excused. However, just as with the work of men, her faults should be considered alongside her work and within the context of history.

Margaret Louise Higgins Sanger changed our world. Born a cheeky little girl in a factory town, she grew up to become a bold woman who led an extraordinary fight against the most powerful opponents in the world: men, the United States government, and the Catholic Church. She succeeded not only in beginning discussions about women's sexuality, sexual health education, reproduction, family planning, and contraception, but also in influencing and affecting the laws to change and improve these basic human rights. The structures she built: the Planned Parenthood Federation of America and the International Planned Parenthood Federation—are still providing sexual and reproductive healthcare and education to almost five million women worldwide.

One hundred and forty years after her birth, Margaret's ideas are still considered controversial. The societal debate over a woman's right to her own body continues to rage today. Choosing to have a baby is both an individual decision and a societal one, just as being human is experienced individually and societally. Each of us balances our individuality against our need to participate in a shared human experience. Maggie spent her life searching out this balance. And in doing so, she helped to move the scales—so weighted against women—a little closer to the center.

Author's Note

This book is a work of fiction. I made it up. This doesn't mean none of this actually happened. It did. "Maggie" Louise Higgins Sanger grew up in Corning, New York, and she lived in that house by the tracks with her very large family. She also hung from the train trestle, washed dishes with her sisters, and helped her father dig up her little brother's grave. Most of the events in this book were pulled straight out of Margaret's autobiography. Some events I combined, and others I reordered for narrative purposes. I recreated Margaret's life as fiction because I wanted to know her better and I wanted you to know her better.

But then why make it up?

The answer is freedom.

I wanted the freedom to combine Margaret's own words found in her autobiography with letters, speeches, newspaper articles, and the accounts of her life as seen through the eyes of the people who knew her and the scholars who studied her.

But to create a breathing, thinking, doing Margaret, I needed the freedom to add to all this my own human sense of who she was as a growing person. Therefore . . . I got to know her as well as anyone can know someone who died before they were born, and then I played Dr. Frankenstein and jolted her alive with the electricity of my imagination.

Selected Bibliography

Printed Sources

Ascher, Carol, Louise DeSalvo, and Sara Ruddick. *Between Women: Biographers, Novelists, Critics, Teachers and Artists Write About Their Work on Women.* Beacon Press, 1984.

Bagge, Peter. *Woman Rebel: The Margaret Sanger Story.* Drawn & Quarterly, 2013.

Baker, Jean H. *Margaret Sanger: A Life of Passion.* Hill and Wang, 2011.

Chesler, Ellen. *Woman of Valor: Margaret Sanger and the Birth Control Movement in America.* Simon & Schuster, 1992.

Engelman, Peter. *A History of the Birth Control Movement in America.* Praeger, 2011.

Katz, Esther, Peter Engelman, Cathy Moran Hajo. *The Selected Papers of Margaret Sanger Volume I: The Woman Rebel, 1900–1928.* University of Illinois Press, 2002.

Epstein, Randi Hutter. *Get Me Out: A History of Childbirth from the Garden of Eden to the Sperm Bank.* W. W. Norton & Company, 2010.

George, Henry. *Progress and Poverty: An Inquiry into the Cause of Industrial Depressions and of Increase Want with Increase of Wealth.* Random House, 1879.

Heilbrun, Carolyn G. *Writing a Woman's Life.* W. W. Norton & Company, 1988.

Owen, Ursula. (Editor) *Fathers: Reflections by Daughters.* Virago Press, 1994.

Sanger, Margaret. *Margaret Sanger: An Autobiography.* W. W. Norton & Company, 1938.

Sanger, Margaret. *My Fight for Birth Control.* Farrar & Rinehart, 1931.

Sanger, Margaret. *The Pivot of Civilization.* Brentano's, 1922.

Sanger, Margaret. *What Every Girl Should Know.* Max N. Maisel, 1916.

Sanger, Margaret. *Women and the New Race.* Brentano's, 1920.

Sprigg, June. *Domestick Beings.* Alfred A. Knopf, 1984.

Newspapers/Periodicals:
The Corning Journal (Weekly), 1847-1905. OCLC 09988334

The Corning Daily Journal (Daily), 189u-19uu. OCLC 25585154

The Corning Democrat (Daily), 1884-1895 OCLC 11655546

Unpublished Manuscript:
Hersey, Harold. Margaret Sanger: *The Biography of the Birth Control Pioneer.* New York, 1938

Acknowledgments

First and foremost, I'd like to express my gratitude to the scholars, historians, and archivists whose dedication in seeking out, preserving, studying, and organizing the life and work of Margaret Sanger provided me the means to write this book. A special thank-you to Peter Engelman of the Margaret Sanger Papers Project at New York University and Smith College for his precious time and boundless expertise. And to Ellen Chesler for inspiring me through her amazing work in *Woman of Valor*. You wrote, "Every woman in the world today who takes her sexual and reproductive autonomy for granted should venerate Margaret Sanger." And because of you, I do.

I'd also like to thank the following local librarians and historians. Details matter. And these are the folks who diligently watch over them. Thank you to Nancy Magrath of the Rakow Research Library in Corning, New York, as well as to Tom Dimitroff and

Peter Foley, local historians in Corning and Claverack, New York, respectively.

If teachers light your way, the following people are bright indeed. Mary Quattlebaum began this work with me as a picture book biography, never dousing the idea with the very real limitations this form would have entailed for my subject. And because of Mary, it grew into a middle grade—where Liz Garton Scanlon took it up with equal gusto, encouraging experimentation while also managing to be a frank editor. Carolyn Yoder stepped in to read it in all its forms, waving me on. And Reka Simonsen, with Julia McCarthy at her side, spent an entire year reshaping it into the book it is today. Dearest Reka, your energy, vision, and patience are astonishing.

Shouting from the sidelines were a host of the most spectacular writing friends. If you think having people along the path rooting for you is no large matter, you've never run a marathon, and surely writing a novel is a marathon. I adore you . . . Cate Berry, Sarah Cassell, Leslie Caulfield, Jennifer Salvato Doktorski, Robin Galbraith, Adrienne Kisner, Carol McAfee, and of course, the Vermont College of Fine Arts Writing for Children and Young Adults's one and only Dead Post-Its Society.

Thanks always to my agent, Kerry Sparks. You are a true partner.

And love to my husband, Kevin Mann, who endured something akin to the torments of hell having to listen to me go on about Margaret Higgins Sanger *for years*.

A final acknowledgment to Margaret Higgins Sanger. So much in my life has been made possible due to your work and dedication. Thank you.